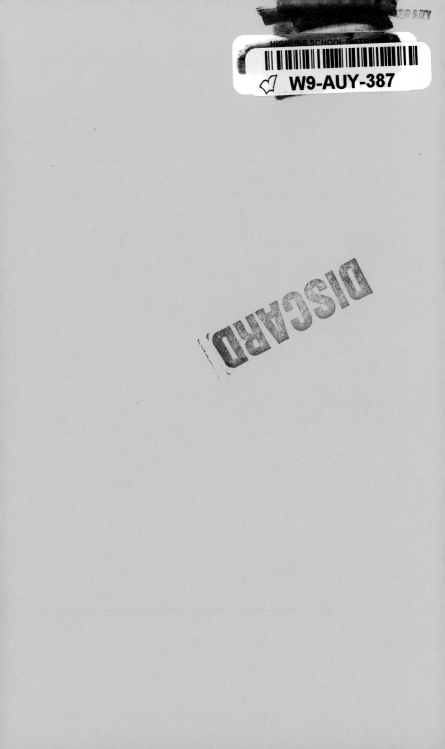

THE LAST
THIRTEEN

BOOK FOUR

JAMES PHELAN

Kane Miller

A DIVISION OF EDC PUBLISHING

PREVIOUSLY

Sam makes a daring escape from the traitorous German Guardians in Italy. Realizing that Xavier is the next of the last 13, Sam and Xavier fly to Berlin to follow Xavier's last 13 dream.

✦

At the archives in Berlin, they find a rubbing of the missing half of Ramses' Dream Stele. Pursued once more by the German Guardians, they flee with Xavier's father, Dr. Dark, who reveals that he is a member of the Dreamer Council.

✦

Eva is at the Academy, working alongside Jedi to unravel the mysteries of the da Vinci journal. They discover a machine called the Bakhu. She dreams of the campfire out on the mountains and goes to investigate. Caught in an avalanche, Eva survives thanks only to an unknown rescuer.

✦

Sam, Xavier and Dr. Dark take refuge at the home of Dr. Dark's associate, Hans. That night, the boys share a nightmare about the next Gear piece. But the next morning,

Hans takes them prisoner, seeking the power of the Dream Gate for himself.

✿

After setting fire to Hans' mansion as they escape, Sam, Xavier and Dr. Dark return to the city to find the Gear piece inside the Berlin Zoo. Dr. Dark leads Hans' men away while Sam and Xavier explore the hidden tunnels under the zoo.

✿

Meanwhile Alex is now working with the Enterprise IT team, alongside his mother, Phoebe. He sneaks aboard Stella's mission to Germany, determined to be involved in the race. He dreams of the zoo and realizes that's where Sam is headed.

✿

Sam and Xavier discover the WWII airplane factory from Xavier's nightmare. Xavier leads them to the Gear piece just as both Stella's rogue Agents and Hans' men arrive, setting off a firefight. The boys escape via an ejector seat but Solaris is waiting for Sam. He struggles to fight back as Solaris looms over him . . .

SAM

This is it. No more outrunning my nightmares.

Sam forced his eyes open, willing himself to face his enemy. Solaris' blackness filled his vision.

"You lose," Solaris growled, his arms stretching out towards Sam.

Sam gritted his teeth and pulled his hands free from the ejector seat to defend himself, pointlessly, bravely. But then—

"Nooooo!" There was a blur of movement and suddenly daylight blinded Sam, and Solaris was gone.

Sam stumbled free from the seat and crashed to the ground, struggling to see what was happening as a gush of hot blood burst out from under his hairline. His vision swam sideways and sticky blood trickled into his left eye . . . *no, no, I have to get the Gear . . . Xavier . . . must get . . .*

And then he passed out.

He blinked his eyes and came to a moment later. Blurry feet rushed towards him.

He rolled onto his back. He tasted blood.

A face filled the sky above him. Someone was close, looking down into his eyes. They looked familiar, those eyes.

Alex?

Then he focused on the mouth. The person was saying something but Sam couldn't hear the words. He tried to talk but wasn't sure if any sound came out. His head turned to the side, and he could see Xavier standing there, dripping wet and shivering. Sam tried to tell them to search for their backpacks.

Who has the Gear?

Sam tilted his head again, but he could not see Solaris.

He must have it; that's why he's gone.

Sam tried to sit up, but he couldn't move.

He saw that familiar face above him talking into a phone.

In a moment of clarity, he knew for certain he was looking at Alex. He tried to smile, to say hello, but he still couldn't talk.

It's Alex. Alex who was dead.

SAM'S NIGHTMARE

The sound of my running footsteps echoes in the huge space. A vaulted ceiling above me reveals no clues. Everything is dark but for tiny night-lights, illuminated exit signs and faint glows on the walls. I slow to a walk, listening. The fear of what may lurk in the gloom is suffocating. I stop.

Be still and listen . . .

Silence.

I let out a breath, feel my heart rate settle. Whatever or whoever was chasing me is no longer there. Maybe they never were . . . I'd been running, but from what—from whom? I'm as unsure about that as I am of my surroundings.

Where am I? Concentrate, Sam. Pay attention.

I walk over to a nearby wall for a closer look. There is an enormous painting set squarely in the middle, smaller pictures hanging on either side, their lamps casting the soft glows I'd noticed. I stagger back from the imposing picture; its sheer size is astounding. It's of a raft adrift at sea, bedraggled men clambering to remain afloat. Desperation and despair leap off the canvas and threaten to overwhelm me.

"Gericault's *The Raft of the Medusa*," a lilting voice says.

I turn. A girl, about my age, stands beside me, studying the huge artwork.

"A magnificent work," she says in a French accent. "But not what you came for."

I'm in France?

"Do I know you?" I ask.

"Zara," she says. "My name is Zara."

"I'm Sam." I look around the empty gallery. "Where is everyone?"

"Follow me," she says and walks away.

We are standing in a restoration room. Zara shows me large glossy printouts.

"This package just arrived," Zara explains. "A long-lost da Vinci project, and now we've found it."

I look at the images.

"I don't see what's important about these," I say. "I mean—important to me, what I'm looking for."

"And what are you looking for?"

"Parts of da Vinci's machine." I keep my voice calm and level.

"He invented many machines." Zara is unflappable.

"This one's special," I insist.

"Aren't they all?" she counters.

"Well . . . this one is called the Bakhu machine. It's a kind of mechanical map, which will reveal the location of somewhere special, a place hidden for a long time."

Now she starts to show some surprise.

"You know of it?" I say.

"I've never heard of the 'Bakhu' but it sounds like you're talking about one of the supposed lost da Vinci navigational devices."

I nod. *Don't let it sound too crazy.*

"They're nothing but da Vinci myth, never verified. A few crude sketches is all that's ever been found."

"The map is real."

"And where would such a 'map' lead?" she asks.

"It leads to a treasure," I say. "A treasure beyond belief."

There is a noise outside. Talking, running—someone searching. I rush over to the door, peer out to the corridor. Shadowy figures rush by.

"We should leave," I say, already looking for an exit. "Someone's out there, in the gallery."

"Security, probably."

"No," I say. "Believe me, they're not security, they're not our friends at all."

"You sure about that?"

I nod and say, "And I know they're after me, and you."

"Who are they—"

"We don't have time, I'll explain later, I promise."

There are voices just outside the door. I look around the room.

Where can we go?

Zara switches off the lights, takes my hand and leads me towards another door at the back of the room, tucked behind some shelves.

"OK," she says as we move fast down a corridor, her voice now panicked. "Say I do dream, that I have seen something that might be part of a machine . . ."

I must have missed something, but this is good. She believes what I'm saying.

"Yes?" I say.

We weave down a passageway then into a larger hall. She stops at a door which is marked SORTIE DE SECOURS.

Zara's face is etched with fear when she says, "Let us say that the dream does not . . . it does not end well. Someone gets hurt."

"Who?" I say. "You? Me?"

"Both of us," she says. "I dreamed that there was a fire, here in the museum, and we couldn't get out."

"Then let's go—" I push the bar which opens the fire escape door.

As we step out, I recoil in horror at the shimmering black figure that greets us, somehow smirking, despite the frozen mask.

Solaris!

We turn to run the other way. I'm pulling her arm, I know

I must be hurting her but we have to get out of here. Her dream is about to come true, sooner than I had expected.

Solaris laughs, a shattering, evil sound that pierces the air as we skid on the polished floor, desperately running.

I'm always running.

Rooms and artworks flash by but I don't dare look back. Zara takes the lead, pulling me here and there, weaving through this maze-like place that she must know so well.

I glimpse the night sky above us, kaleidoscoping through a pyramid of glass.

We've almost made it out . . .

Zara drags me towards the exit. It's within reach when blackness shoots up on all sides. I'm spinning, turning, but it's a circle of evil.

Solaris is all around us. How can this be?

Zara's eyes are wide in terror and her mouth opens as if to scream. Before any noise comes out, there's a bright flash from a jet of flames that illuminates the stars above us for the briefest of moments. I turn to Zara as our world—

Explodes.

SAM

Sam woke up panting for breath, the bedsheets twisted around his body. The warm sunlight streamed through the window and spilled over his face. He lay still, calming himself.

It's just another nightmare . . . I can do this. I even got a name this time. Zara.

Squinting against the light, he could see out the window to the Swiss Alps, stretching away to the horizon. It was early morning at the Academy. Sam sighed.

In a seat in a dark corner of the room was a sleeping figure. In the shadows, Sam couldn't make out who it was. When he sat up to see, his head went spinning back to the pillow.

Something wasn't right.

This . . . this isn't my bedroom.

"Ah, you're awake," Lora said, entering the room. The Academy's doctor followed her in. "How are you feeling?"

I'm in the medical bay.

"Not too bad," Sam said, "except for a cracking headache." The figure in the corner stirred. *Eva.*

"Hey," Sam said to her as she walked over, rubbing the sleep from her face as she struggled to fully wake up.

"Hey, you," Eva said. "You had us worried."

"Yeah, sorry about that," Sam said. "How'd I get here?"

"You spent a night at a hospital in Berlin, then we airlifted you back here," Lora said. "You've been out of it for about forty-eight hours."

"Berlin?"

"You don't remember?"

Sam strained to recall.

"What do you last remember?" the doctor asked carefully.

"I remember . . . Solaris?" Sam said. "I was . . . I was at the zoo, in Berlin. I was falling, or flying, coming at him from above, I was gliding down—and then . . ."

"Then?"

"I hit the ground, hard. I remember seeing fire and then I blacked out . . . it feels like it was all a dream."

"Well, it definitely happened," Lora said. "You were caught up in a shoot-out in the underground factory there and made a rather spectacular escape via an ejection seat."

"*That*, I remember!" Sam said, sitting up and staying up this time. "I was with Xavier—is he OK?"

"Yes, he's fine, just a bit shaken up. He'll be joining us at the Academy soon. We thought he could do with spending a bit longer recuperating with his father first."

Sam nodded. *He needs some time with his dad.*

"And the Gear?" he asked.

Lora shook her head. "Solaris has it."

"No . . ." Sam's vision wobbled again and he leaned back heavily in the bed.

"Just sit still a moment," the doctor said, checking Sam's vital signs. "You suffered a concussion and the lump on your head will be there for a while. Four stitches. Might I suggest that you refrain from using World War II ejection seats in future?"

Sam nodded again but felt absent as a niggling memory remained just out of reach.

"Sam?" Eva said, standing close to him and recognizing his confusion. "What is it?"

"Alex!" Sam said, the memory of his face flooding back. "I saw Alex there, at the zoo!" Sam said, growing more and more lucid with every second that he was awake. "I saw *Alex*, I know it. He's alive!"

"It's OK, Sam," Lora said, sitting on the edge of his bed. "Jedi had online photographic searches running following the plane wreck in New York and he found a match for Alex a few days ago in Berlin. It looks as though he was there with the Enterprise. We don't know why they would have taken him along on a mission like that though."

"That's right, the Enterprise were there too," Sam said. "They were after us—after the Gear!"

"Are you saying that Alex is *working* for the Enterprise?" Eva said. "Why would he do that?"

"Well, if Alex has been with the Enterprise since the . . . accident in New York . . ." Lora's voice still wavered at the mention of the jet explosion that had killed her boyfriend, Sebastian.

"If Alex is still alive," Eva said, "maybe Sebastian and Tobias are too?"

Sam could see that the thought was playing on Lora's mind. She went to the window and looked outside, quiet as Eva began to tell Sam how she'd been stuck out in the mountains outside the Academy and how an avalanche had nearly swept her away.

"I think Tobias carried me back here," Eva said. "At first I thought it was just a dream, but maybe I really did see him . . ."

"Maybe," Lora admitted. "The day after you were brought back following your hike out there, I sent a team out to the mountain. They didn't find anyone, but they did find this." Lora pulled out a dream catcher charm and placed it on the table in front of Sam.

"It belonged to Tobias," Lora said.

"Then it *is* him!" Eva said.

"Eva, if it is Tobias, which it may or may not be, he's there for a reason. And unless he—or whoever it is—comes to us, we won't know. It's impossible to find someone out there if they don't want to be found."

"Wow, this is getting bizarre." Sam looked to Eva and Lora, both nervous and tense. "In other news," he said, taking the IV line out of his arm and getting up, as the doctor began muttering and trying to get him back into the bed, "I know where I have to go."

"Oh?" Lora said. Both she and Eva were immediately intrigued and alert.

Sam smiled. "I've had my next dream."

ALEX

"**Y**ou can't do that again," Phoebe said to Alex. They were sitting on a plaza bench in downtown San Jose, local people out enjoying a weekend street fair mingling around them.

"Do what?" Alex said, already knowing the answer. "Eat another bag of these delicious jam doughnuts?"

"Stowing away," his mother said with a stern tone. "Sneaking along on a mission like that. You could have gotten yourself, and others, hurt or even killed. Did you think it'd be easier to ask for forgiveness after the fact than to get permission to go out there?"

"Sorry, Mom. But I can take care of myself, you know," Alex said. "Besides, Sam's out there 'in the field,'" Alex made sarcastic quotation marks in the air with his hands, "and everyone seems to trust him to know what he's doing."

"I'm sure the Academy would prefer to avoid that if they could," Phoebe said.

"But I don't get it," Alex said, licking sugar from his fingers and scrunching up the empty paper bag. "Sam's out there risking his neck for us, and he needs all the help he can get. Meanwhile, I'm stuck here, hanging out with the world's greatest concentration of geeks."

"The Enterprise is doing everything it can to—"

"I think the Enterprise has you brainwashed, Mom," he said. "Do you even know what's going on out there? Really? Sam's up against Solaris, with all kinds of people chasing him, *shooting* at him, and we're here, sitting around, talking, watching, *waiting*."

"I've told you, there are rules here. You need to speak to the director about going out with the teams."

"Yeah, well, I will," Alex said, standing up from the bench and tossing the bag in a nearby trash can. He turned to face his mother. "How do you even know we can trust this director guy anyway? From what I saw in Berlin, Stella *isn't* playing by the rules. I *know* I heard Solaris talking to her, giving her orders. I don't understand why we're not in there," he pointed to the gleaming skyscraper behind him, "telling the big boss about it right now!"

"You know why. He's not here—he was called away for an urgent meeting and this is something we need to discuss with him in person. He'll be back later. And I promise you we *can* trust him. I've worked with Jack for a long time, Alex," she said. "Some of his methods may seem a bit drastic, but he always operates with integrity."

"Well, I think he needs to know that Stella is working *against* him—against all of us. And *with* Solaris!" Alex added. "I mean, who knows what she'll do next?"

"We *will* tell Jack, I promise," Phoebe said, standing up and putting an arm around her son, "the first chance we get. But we need to be sure we won't be overheard."

"In case Stella realizes I discovered her secret?" he asked.

"Exactly. We need to wait until the time is right so we can grab her *and* all her accomplices. And Alex?"

"Yeah?"

"I just want to say again how proud I am that you helped save Sam. And that you were able to play along with Stella all the way back here. I always knew you were smart *and* brave."

Alex reddened and looked away, suddenly shy.

"Another bag of doughnuts?" Phoebe said, laughing to break the tension. "Come on, I know you want some more." Phoebe took his arm and Alex smiled as they headed across to the vendor. "And feel free to share this time, won't you?"

In a small office on the twentieth floor of the Enterprise building, Alex was scanning news footage from the gunfight at the Berlin Zoo. The current snippet showed a news reporter explaining that more details, including new unseen footage, would be available soon.

I know Stella was there. I heard her open fire on Sam, but I need proof. I have to make Jack believe me.

Phoebe sat next to Alex, squinting at the flickering screen.

"That's where I saw Sam," Alex said to his mother, pointing at the monitor. "Solaris too."

"I thought you said Solaris was with Stella?"

"No, he was talking to her over a radio receiver. Giving orders. But then he came up above ground to find Sam. If I'd had one of those Tasers or a dart gun, I could have taken him."

"I think you did amazingly well to fight him off as you did. All the more because you *didn't* have a weapon," Phoebe said. "But don't underestimate Solaris. He's ruthless. We're fortunate he decided to run instead of staying to fight."

"But he got whatever it was that Sam and Xavier must have been looking for. So it was all for nothing," Alex sighed.

"Not for nothing. You all survived to fight another day and the battle is far from over. Solaris is driven by the desire to win the race, find whatever it is that is at the end," Phoebe said, sitting next to her son. "And he'll do *anything* to make that happen."

Alex didn't respond.

"You, me, we don't matter to him," she said. "He'd think nothing of swatting us out of the way, or destroying an airliner, a school, an entire city, if it got him closer to his objective."

"Then we have to stop him," Alex said. "Someone has to."

"It's not that easy," Phoebe said. "No one knows *who* he

is, never mind where he is."

"Why don't we find out more about him, find out who our enemy really is?"

Phoebe shook her head. "We've tried," she said. "Many have tried, for decades, to predict who Solaris would be. All of this—the last 13 Dreamers, the evil of Solaris—has been prophesied for centuries."

"How can he just appear like this?"

"The same way the 13 are appearing because the time is right. Solaris is the shadow of all that is good. And all that the 13 represent, he's the opposite of that."

"Do you think Solaris is a Dreamer like us?"

"I don't know. No one knows."

The news clip in the background had run into a sports bulletin, the reporter animatedly discussing the latest scores. Alex tuned out as the report went on in the background.

The world has no clue about the war raging around them, right now, right under their noses.

"Well, *someone* out there knows more about Solaris than we do," Alex said. "Stella."

SAM

When Sam walked into the Academy's dining hall for lunch, the assembled students erupted into cheers, calling out to congratulate him and welcome him back. The sound was deafening for a moment as everyone's attention turned to Sam.

Don't they know I lost the Gear?

Sam felt himself turn red, and he gave an awkward wave and sat down at his usual table. Eva was there, along with a handful of other students. Finally, the noise dropped to a hum of talking and laughter.

"Hey, Sam," Pi said, sitting forward and looking eager.

"Hey, Pi," Sam said, then turned to Eva and asked, "have you seen Gabriella?"

"Me? Why, because we're roomies now?" Eva asked with an arched eyebrow. "Look, if you must know, she's over there." She pointed across the room to where Gabriella was surrounded by starstruck students. "Hanging out with her adoring fans."

"Oh yeah," Sam said, watching Gabriella hold court.

Eva rolled her eyes and continued eating.

"We haven't had that many pop stars here," Pi said. "Personally, I don't know what the fuss is about," he added with a shy smile at Eva. Sam noticed Pi blush as he turned to him and said, "So, Sam, we heard about Berlin—Italy too. Sounds like you're doing awesome."

"Thanks, Pi," Sam said to his first-year friend.

"I mean, you *beat* Solaris," Pi gushed, fidgeting with the bright-red glasses on the bridge of his nose. "Do you realize how amazing that is?"

"I got *lucky*," Sam said. "Once. The second time—not so much." Sam pointed to the gauze on his forehead and the spray-on bandage on his grazed forearm.

"Battle scars," Pi said, smiling and taking a photo with his phone. "So epic! I'm going to update the school newsletter with these. Everyone's keen to hear all about you."

"Newsletter?"

"Yeah! I can see the headline now—'Hero defeats villain, but then gets beaten. The score is one-all, but Sam is ready to fight another day!' Cool, right?"

"Yeah, well, it doesn't feel very cool," Sam said. "And, really, do we need an update about me for the school's newsletter?"

"Absolutely," Pi nodded, his fingers already tapping at his smartphone screen.

He turned the screen to show Sam. "It'll be very flattering, don't worry!"

The Echo

The Academy Newsletter

THE
ACADEMY
mens agitat molem

Issue 26

≳insert heading≲
Hero defeats villain – then gets beaten

≳insert subheading≲
Score is one-all but Sam is ready to fight another day!

≳body text≲
≳image≲
≳footer≲
≳notes≲

Sam's face fell.

Oh man, now I'm some kind of poster boy for Dreamers?

"You should eat something," Eva said to Sam, changing the subject. "I'm getting some more lunch, want some?"

"Um, yeah, sure . . ." Sam said.

"Hi, Sam," singsong voices called out behind him.

He turned to find twin girls from his year standing there, carrying a plate of cupcakes on a tray.

"Red velvet cupcakes," one said.

"We made them," said the other.

"For you." They both slapped Pi's hand as he tried reaching for a cupcake.

"*Just* for you, Sam."

Both girls smiled at Sam, expectant looks on their faces.

Sam flushed a deeper shade of red at all this unwanted attention.

"Ah, thanks," he said, taking a cupcake decorated with an image of himself and took a bite. "Wow, delicious. Eva, you should try one."

"No thanks," Eva said, her look ticking off the girls.

"I'll have one," Pi said, reaching out only to have his hand slapped away again. "Well, that's just rude!" he muttered.

"Ah, well, thanks," Sam said, taking the plate from the girls, who ran away giggling.

"Why is it that all schools are the same? Even this one?" Eva said to Sam while she looked at the cupcakes on the plate in front of them.

"C'mon, Eva, it's not that bad," Sam said, passing one to Pi. "They're just trying to be nice."

"Fine," Eva said, sighing. She took a cupcake and bit into it. "OK, these are pretty amazing," she mumbled through a mouthful of frosting.

Sam's phone bleeped with a message from Lora.

The Professor is ready to see you in his office.

"Gotta go," Sam said, standing. "You coming, Eva?"

"You're sure?" she said.

"Sure as you just smashed that cupcake in like five seconds flat."

"Can I come too?" Pi asked.

"Sorry, dude, next time," Sam said.

"That's what you always say!" Pi said, putting down his cupcake and adding more text to his phone. "I'm adding that to your list of catchphrases."

"What catchphrases? I have a list of catchphrases?"

"Yup," Pi said. "Such as, 'drive it like you stole it,' 'let's roll,' 'it's time to save the world again . . .'"

"I don't think I've ever said any of those things," Sam said.

"His favorite catchphrase is 'what catchphrases?'" Pi dictated to himself as he typed. "Update done." He looked up at Sam and smiled.

"Well," Sam said, giving Pi a friendly bump on the shoulder, "I'm sure there'll be plenty of time for you to step up to the plate—so be ready."

Sam and Eva walked out, and Pi called after them, "Let's roll!"

"**G**reat to see you up and about," the Professor said to Sam.

Sam and Eva entered the office to find the Professor waiting for them. Tall and lean with wispy gray hair, he was leaning on his desk, watching a huge wall-mounted screen. Lora and Jedi stood with a tablet computer between them, bringing up details that Sam recognized immediately.

"Hey, Sam, as you were kind enough to have your 'last 13' dream here at the Academy this time, we were able to record it and I've even ID'd the next Dreamer," Jedi said, bringing up an image on the monitor.

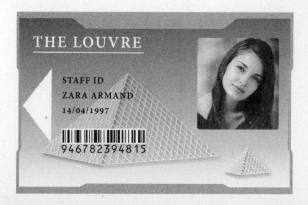

THE LOUVRE

STAFF ID
ZARA ARMAND
14/04/1997

946782394815

"Ta-da! This is Zara, aged sixteen, living in Paris."

"That's her," Sam said. He walked up to the screen and looked at the image close-up. "Wow—she's in high school *and* working at the Louvre museum?" He looked around at Jedi. "How did you find her so fast?"

"Because I'm a genius," Jedi grinned. "That, plus we had her first name and we could assume she worked at the Louvre. It was simply a matter of zipping into their database, ahem, and running the names until we had a match. There aren't many teenagers called Zara working there."

"I'm still impressed, Jedi. Really."

Jedi beamed as the Professor clapped him on the back.

"And that's not all we found out," Lora continued, flicking through Zara's personal details. "Thanks to our friend at the Enterprise, we know that her parents are both Agents with cover jobs in the arts," Lora said.

Jedi brought up images of the two people who'd raised Zara, along with their Enterprise employment history.

Good old Shiva.

"Her father, Mr. Armand, is a lecturer at the Sorbonne," Lora continued.

"That's the famous university in Paris, right?" Sam asked.

"Yes," Lora said. "He's a specialist in da Vinci. And her mother . . . let's see. Her mother works as an art conservationist at the Louvre. Which would explain Zara working there."

"Anything else useful come out from my dream?" Sam asked.

"Not so far, but I'll keep working on it—I'm currently researching a way to tap into the parts of the dream that get skipped or passed over," Jedi said. "So watch this space."

"So, what's our next step?" Lora said to the Professor.

"We will go straight to Paris and meet with Zara," the Professor said. "We'll see if she's had her dream and hope that she already knows where to go to find her Gear."

"You don't think it's getting too dangerous for Sam?" Lora said. "We could have local Guardians bring her here."

"I'm afraid there's no time for that," the Professor said, looking to Sam. "Sam should be there to meet each of the 13—he has parts of the same dream, he may need to help them remember it. And it could even be that we'll be closer to where we need to be, as with Gabriella in Rome. Then we can act swiftly and try to stay ahead in the race."

Lora nodded, knowing it made sense, then said, "But Sam's injuries from Berlin . . ."

"I'm fine," Sam said.

The Professor looked from those in the room to the window, lost for a moment in the view.

"Professor?" Sam said.

"We'll go to Paris—just Sam and I, and have the local French Guardians meet us there," he said, turning back to face everyone. "That'll give me an opportunity to meet with the Council of Dreamers, and find out what we can do about shutting down Hans and the German Guardians. This race is getting more dangerous every day and we must be more proactive in the fight."

Lora did not look pleased at the thought of staying behind.

"I'll need you here, Lora," the Professor said. "There are troubling times ahead, and I need you to make sure the students remain safe. And Xavier is due to arrive at the Academy tomorrow. You should be here to welcome him."

Lora nodded. "And what about Stella and her Enterprise team who were at the zoo?" she asked. "The Council must take action against the Enterprise to shut them down."

"And they were in New York too," Sam added, "when Stella pretended to *be* Solaris."

"Yes," the Professor said, packing his briefcase. "I'll see what kind of pressure the Council can bring to bear on these rogue elements. Unfortunately, I think we will find that the race will bring with it new enemies that we are powerless to stop with sanctions and regulations."

"You're packing your things now?" Sam asked. "I mean—we're leaving straightaway?"

The Professor smiled. "You're not ready?"

"Sure, of course I am," Sam asserted.

"Good," the Professor said. "We leave in an hour."

"Let's roll!" Sam said.

Eva leaned over and whispered to him, "Pi was right. You really do say that a lot."

"I think I should go with you," Eva said as she left the Professor's office with Sam, headed for the dorm wing.

"No, too many people make it hard to get around unnoticed," Sam said. "You might end up getting in the way."

Eva stopped mid-stride, staring at him with burning eyes.

"Hang on, not *you* . . ." Sam added hastily but Eva had already turned on her heel and walked away without another word.

"Eva, you know I don't mean . . ." Sam called out to her, but it was too late.

Man, that's really not what I meant to say.

"Sam?"

"Yeah?" Sam said, turning around to face Jedi. "Zup?"

"Can I show you something?" he said.

"I've got to get ready," Sam said, his eyes downcast. "You heard the Professor."

"Five minutes?" Jedi said, hopeful. "I mean, you'll be wearing your Stealth Suit, so what's to pack—a toothbrush?"

Sam laughed and said, "OK, sure, lead the way."

Down in the rock-hewn computer lair, carved deep into the mountain, lights flashed on ahead of them as they walked. In Jedi's glass-walled office jutting out over the supercomputer floor, Sam saw two things laid out on a table—a Stealth Suit and a smartphone.

"Ta-da!" Jedi said with a wave of his hands. "You like?"

"Ah, I already have these," Sam said.

"Not like this, you don't," Jedi said with a huge grin.

Sam looked at the items again. "They're . . . different somehow?"

"Newer models," Jedi said. "This is a *Third* Gen Suit, specially formulated to work in sync with your neuro— ah, the technical aspects don't matter. It fits like a glove and adapts at will, all that usual stuff, plus a bit more. I've already uploaded your neural pathways as mapped by the dream machine, so it'll work straightaway. No more glitching or trying to work out how to make the changes. Just think it and it'll do it."

"Awesome!" Sam said. The Stealth Suits, crafted out of a memory-technology fabric and worn by Academy field staff, changed appearances and textures at the will of the user. The thing was, it could take up to a year to figure out how to control them precisely and Sam didn't have the luxury of that kind of training time.

Although Eva got the hang of these things real quick.

Eva . . . huh.

"And what's with the phone?" Sam refocused on the table in front of him.

"This," Jedi said, picking up what looked just like a typical phone, "I call my 'add-on' package." He flicked through some apps. "I've uploaded a few of my own design, as well as some that I 'borrowed' from the US military—like this one, for example."

He flicked off the lights in the room, showing Sam how the app turned the phone's camera lens into a night vision device.

"Bit more powerful and functional than your typical app," Jedi said.

"That's ten kinds of awesome!" Sam said, looking at the screen which showed the world around them lit up like twilight. It was able to zoom in to span a considerable distance and pick up details across the vast computer room next door.

"And this," he said, flicking through to another function, "is thermal imaging."

There was a red-orange and yellow flaring of Sam's hand as he passed it under the camera lens.

Jedi brought the office lights up again.

"Similar to X-ray, it will pass through solid objects up to about a foot and a half, like through thick walls, say."

"That's . . . handy."

"Another app on here . . . where is it . . . converts over

a hundred languages in and out of English in real time."
Jedi flipped through the pages of app screens. "I'll let you
find that. And last but not least, is *this*. Use this app as
an absolute last resort because it will fry your phone." Jedi
pushed on another app and little sharp prongs poked out
the bottom of the handset. "A Taser-type device. It'll knock
someone out cold—but it'll kill your battery, so be wary,
it's a once-only number until you recharge the handset.
For self-defense, of course."

"Of course." Sam reset the phone and pocketed it. "OK,
I'd better go pack my toothbrush."

"Sam?"

"Yeah?"

"Good luck out there," Jedi said, rolling up the Stealth
Suit for him.

"Thanks, man," Sam said.

"See you on the flip side," Jedi called out as Sam left.

Sam couldn't find Eva to say good-bye. He left her a note,
slung his backpack over his shoulder and headed outside.
The snow was being blown horizontally and Sam thought
about how cold it was. Almost instantly he felt his new
Stealth Suit change to become a big puffy snow suit. *Nice!*

He pulled open the Suit for a moment—making one
last check of the precious key that hung once more around

his neck. "I don't know why," he'd told the Professor, "but I just know I need it with me." He was so grateful that the Professor had just nodded and returned the key to him. Sam smiled to himself to think of the trust the Professor now had in him.

I hope I can show him, and everyone else, that I'm up to the job.

He ran over to the helicopter, its rotors beginning to turn in the thin mountain air, to find the Professor already strapped into a seat in the back. Sam gave him the thumbs-up. As they slowly rose into the sky, he watched the tile roof of the Academy through the window until it faded out of sight.

ALEX

"I'll show them I'm ready," Alex said to himself as he ran on a treadmill in the Enterprise's gym. "I'll be more ready than anyone."

He ran flat out, as fast as he could, until he had to jump off in exhaustion.

"Looked like you were going to run through the wall," a familiar voice said.

"Yeah . . ." Alex replied, seeing Shiva across the room. "Trying to get fitter. Get bigger guns. Maybe some rippling abs."

"Uh-huh, good luck with all that."

"Thanks," Alex said, draining his water bottle. "That's some outfit you're wearing."

"Was due for a match," Shiva said, dressed in white fencing gear, a helmet in one hand and a thin-bladed sword in the other. "But my partner has dropped out."

"Fencing, eh?" Alex said, wiping the sweat from his face with a hand towel. "Always wanted to try that."

"Why not step in?"

"Step in? Like, now?"

"Sure, I'll go easy on you. Then again, with those bulging biceps, maybe you should go easy on me."

"OK." Alex followed Shiva over to the gym clerk who got Alex fitted out with all the gear. He took the sword and swished it around in the air.

"It's an épée," Shiva said as he led them into the arena. "The electronic tip will record the hits, and the entire body is a valid target area. And there's no taking turns like you get with other fencing. This is just 'game on.'"

"Even the gloves are a target?" Alex said, pulling his gloves on.

"Even the gloves," Shiva said. "In fact, the glove of the épée hand is a good target because it's always close."

"How'd you get into this?" Alex said, putting on his mask.

"Because of my work in IT," Shiva said, taking guard. "Working for Matrix in his computer lab—believe me, a couple years of working for that guy, you need to do something like this."

"He can't be that bad," Alex scoffed. "Isn't he just your normal genius-computer-guru weirdo?"

"Our supervisor," Shiva said, "is one of the smartest guys on the planet—he went from being a fifteen-year-old high-school student in Taiwan to running his own software company at twenty. The director met him and lured him here with a huge salary and even cooler toys to play with."

"Is that why he never leaves the lab and is so secretive about what he's doing?"

"Probably," Shiva said, stretching out his arms and legs and getting ready. "Matrix wouldn't bother to explain his work to me. Ready?"

"I think so," Alex said, standing opposite.

"OK, stand like this, see?"

Alex tried to copy Shiva's stance, bending his legs into a standing squat.

"Excellent. Now, try moving forward in an advance, like this."

Alex followed Shiva's move.

"And bring your back leg in front of your front leg, so you can sprint past your opponent. We can work on that next time."

"Ha! What makes you think there'll be a next time?" Alex said, slashing at the air with his sword.

"You're confident, that's good," Shiva said. "Mind you don't attack like that though, these aren't sabers. With épées, it's a pointed attack with the tip only. Ready?"

"Yep."

"En-garde!"

Before Alex knew it, Shiva lunged at him and hit him in the chest. The buzzer whined and a number one lit up on the scoreboard.

"Ah, I see how we're playing . . ." Alex said, settling back to his starting position.

"En-garde!"

Another hit, this time on Alex's bicep.

"In fairness," Shiva said, a smile in his voice, "it was a big target!"

"Right, I got this . . ." Alex said, concentrating on his moves.

"En-garde!"

3–0, Shiva got Alex on the forearm.

4–0, another hit on the hand this time.

"OK," Alex said, "I think I'm getting the hang of it now . . ."

It was 12–0 when Alex scored a hit on Shiva's glove.

"Aha!" Alex exclaimed, bowing to his opponent. "I think I have this mastered."

Alex won the next two and they finished up 15–3, the second bout going 15–6.

"A final bout?" Shiva said. He was smiling, having hardly broken a sweat.

"Maybe tomorrow?" Alex said, his legs burning from half an hour of parrying and lunging.

"Sure," Shiva said, slipping off his mask and tilting his head in respect. "I think with my training, you may prove to be a worthy opponent in no time."

"Opponent shmopponent," Alex said, following Shiva out of the room. "Give it a few lessons and I'll be kicking your butt back to your computer chair."

SAM

"**H**ave you been to Paris before?" the Professor asked as their car moved through the busy streets of the city. A van-load of local Guardians rode close behind them.

"No," Sam replied. "I visited France with my family when I was ten. We stayed on the south coast where my dad was attending a conference, but we didn't come to Paris."

"Hmm, well, I think you'll like it," the Professor replied. "Plenty to see, plenty to do. A real one of a kind."

Sam looked at the Professor's face as he watched out the window with a glint of wonder in his eyes. He was maybe sixty or so, his wispy gray hair and eyebrows making him look like an Einstein poster Sam remembered from the back of the science lab door at school.

I wonder if he's spent his whole life waiting for this moment, hoping for it. And now we're close to getting to the Dream Gate and whatever power is beyond it.

"Here we are," the Professor said, interrupting Sam's thoughts. "Our hotel."

Sam had his own room in the suite, the brawny Guardians setting up station in the adjoining room. He flicked on the television in the living room and found an international news station. The Professor came in from his bedroom, now dressed smartly as if going to a formal occasion.

"Fancy clothes for a fancy hotel?" Sam said.

The Professor smiled and said, "This place is owned by a member of the Council."

"And what's the plan?" Sam asked the Professor. "You look like you're ready for your senior prom."

"Ha, well, I must go to a function, where I will meet with the chairman of the Council," the Professor said, "to prepare for our meeting with the full Council tomorrow."

"Hey, look," Sam said, turning up the volume on the newscast on the television.

A reporter was at the Berlin Zoo, showing viewers the WWII aircraft found in the underground assembly plant.

"Least they're not talking about me," Sam said.

"And now we will show you some images from the event, as yet unreleased to the public," the reporter said.

The images changed to footage from the events three days before—the explosion that Stella's forces set off, enabling them to rappel into the underground bunker.

"That was her," Sam said. "That had to have been Stella!"

"Jedi's checked the footage from security cameras in the zoo," the Professor said. "There were no images to identify them for certain."

"Yeah, well, she's a smart operator, we know that."

The news feed switched back to the reporter.

"This area of the zoo is still off-limits," the newscaster said. "As for reports from zoo patrons of hearing a gunfight, authorities are being tight-lipped, saying that they are looking into the situation. What's certain though is that two teenagers were shot into the sky via a World War II-era ejection seat, as captured in this tourist video."

Sam watched as he and Xavier went rocketing up into the air.

"Gotta admit, it looks pretty cool on TV . . ." Sam said. He winced when he saw the fire shoot past his falling figure.

"Their identities, as with all involved, are still unknown, including this mysterious masked figure in black."

"Solaris!" Sam said, pointing at the screen. He shook his head in disbelief. It was beyond surreal to see the apparition from his nightmares on the screen.

The footage shifted to slow motion as Solaris bent down and took something from Sam. The resolution was too low to make it out.

"That's when he took the Gear," Sam said. Then Solaris paused over Sam's unconscious body—*what was he thinking, why did he leave me unharmed?*

No sooner had Sam had that thought when the answer was presented to him. A loud, piercing *"Nooo!"* could be heard off screen and then suddenly another figure ran into view, hurtling towards Solaris.

Solaris turned and slammed his arm into his would-be attacker as they both staggered out of the camera frame. When the camera panned back, Solaris was gone.

That must have been Alex.

Wow, he totally saved me from Solaris.

"And what we see here is that there may have been a third teenager involved," the reporter said. "Again, due to the amateur nature of the footage, it's impossible to get an ID on any of the parties involved. Police are calling for witnesses to come forward . . ."

"That was Alex!" Sam said, looking to the Professor, who watched on quietly.

"Interpol has confirmed that a worldwide manhunt is underway for all parties concerned and that it is just a matter of time until they are apprehended."

The reporter signed off and then it went back to the news anchor.

"Well," Sam said to the Professor. "I guess that could have been worse."

The Professor pointed to the screen.

"This just in, an image of the unconscious teen from the Berlin Zoo incident, taken by a news photographer who was one of the first to arrive at the scene."

Sam swallowed hard. The photo was of a bleeding and battered face, but he knew it well—it was *his* face.

EVA

Eva finished her classes for the day and sat with Gabriella and Xavier in one of the Academy rec rooms. Xavier had arrived earlier that morning and seemed to be really embracing his role in the last 13 race.

"I'm going mad without my stylist," Gabriella said in her Italian-accented English as she looked at her reflection in a mirror. "And I'm not used to getting homework again!" She made a face and Xavier laughed.

Will I be like Xavier and Gabriella? I don't feel like one of the last 13. Maybe I am just like the rest of the students here, an ordinary Dreamer.

"Yeah, well, I'd be happier on the road with Sam again. Don't get me wrong, this place seems really cool and everything," Xavier said, pacing, "but surely we can just come back if the Academy needs us."

"What about Dr. Dar—I mean, your dad?" Eva asked. "Don't you want to be with him?"

"He's always been busy doing his own thing and I can't see that changing much now, last 13 or not," Xavier said. "I mean, he made out it was nice to spend time together after all the craziness in Berlin, but he was pretty quick to have me dropped off here. Who knows where he is now . . ."

Eva and Gabriella exchanged an awkward look.

"I'm sure he's just looking out for you," Eva countered.

Xavier shrugged.

"I wish I had someone looking out for me," Eva murmured to herself.

"OK then, so what would you be doing out there, with Sam?" Gabriella asked brightly.

"What would I do?" Xavier said, scratching his chin. "I'd be backing him up, taking care of bad guys." He winked back at Gabriella, who rolled her eyes.

Sam might not want you there. I can't believe he didn't want me to go with him . . .

"On this I agree with Xavier," Gabriella said, getting to her feet. "We should go, the three of us, and do what we can to—"

"There you are," Lora said, hurrying into the room. She seemed slightly out of breath as though she'd run there. "There's been a complication, with Sam."

"Is he OK?" Eva asked, getting to her feet and feeling panic rise inside her.

"Yes, but his activities in Berlin didn't go unnoticed," Lora said. She explained the news bulletins and the images of Sam being circulated across the globe. "The whole world's going to be looking for him now. He's being portrayed as some kind of fugitive."

"What can we do?" Eva said.

"You can help Jedi turn the online tide," Lora said. "He needs the three of you to join him in the computer labs."

Eva didn't need to be asked twice—she ran all the way to Jedi's office with Xavier and Gabriella right behind her.

"Like this?" Eva asked, clicking on the image of Sam on the computer screen.

"That's it," Jedi said. "As my search brings up all the images from news services and the Internet, you guys swap the pics like I showed you."

"Got it," Xavier replied, replacing an image on a web page with a doctored version which no longer resembled Sam.

CLASSIFIED VS UNCLASSIFIED

WHO IS THE MYSTERY BOY?

The conspiracy sphere is abuzz with reports of a teenage boy, aged between 15–18 years old, who has popped up in running battles both in Rome and now in the middle of the Berlin Zoo.

Could he be some European underage crime lord? Or perhaps a superspy on a secret mission? In any case, he's certainly caught the attention of the media and the international police, all of whom are eager to snare an interview with this elusive youth.

Do you know more? Who do you think he is? Who is he working for?

Share your views and news with *Classfied vs. Unclassified*.

villain or hero?

COMMENT

"You think we can get all the images on the net?" Eva asked.

"We can but try," Jedi said. "It's a fresh news story and hasn't gotten much traction outside Western Europe yet."

"I wish I had this program before," Gabriella said, switching the images of Sam on the *International Herald Tribune* web page. "There are so many pictures of me that are just . . . *eurgh*." She made a fake vomiting face and Eva couldn't help but giggle.

"I find that hard to believe," Xavier said, a little too quickly. "I mean, that you could, like, take a bad photo, you know."

"Gross!" Eva said, and Gabriella and Jedi laughed.

"What?" Xavier said. "I was being nice. *What?*"

They were all still laughing as Eva switched Sam's pic on the *Washington Post* site. "Come on guys," she said, "work faster!"

SAM

The Professor left for his function, and Sam stood by a window, watching the Paris street below fill with life as workers left their jobs for the day. It had rained, briefly, and the cobblestones were reflecting the low afternoon sun. Through the open window the sound and fury of rush hour rose up to him.

I'm glad I didn't need to go along to some boring black-tie ball. I'll leave the talking and negotiating to the Professor, thanks very much. What I can *do is find Zara before the bad guys show up and ruin the party again.*

Sam continued to talk himself into racing out the door. He trusted the Professor and knew he was right to ask Sam to wait in the hotel room. But a part of him felt that he was wasting time, and giving up a chance to make his next move unnoticed.

Eva—I hope you're OK, he texted into his phone. **Stay safe, contact me any time.**

Sam paced the room. Flicking through the TV channels, he saw that he was still on some of the news channels and turned it off. He stood at the window again.

I shouldn't be here like this, waiting. It's so busy down there, No one will notice me. I could go out incognito . . .

Sam stood before a full-length mirror. At his whim, his appearance changed to jeans and a T-shirt with a loose-fitting red jacket. He changed again and in the blink of an eye he was wearing a plain dark suit like many he'd spied out the window. That'd be a good way to blend in if he had to ditch any pursuers. He changed back to the casual clothes.

One thing he couldn't change was his face. He remembered that photo from the news—*how many Parisians might have seen that pic by now?* He went to the bathroom and slicked down his hair, brushing it in a new style with a side part. Sam slipped on his sunglasses and scrawled a quick note about going out sightseeing before heading for the door.

Time to go. Destiny is waiting . . .

In the hallway outside his room the coast was clear. Sam knew that the Guardians in the adjoining room were there in case anyone made it up to the floor. The guys on lookout were downstairs, plain-clothed in their own Stealth Suits, keeping watch.

He took the stairs instead of the elevator, figuring there'd be less chance of security cameras. This hotel was owned by a member of the Dreamer Council, so no doubt the Guardians would have someone posted in the security room too, watching all the monitors.

It's all for my safety—so why does this feel like I'm breaking out of prison?

In the lobby he kept out of sight, just inside the stairwell. Across in the lounge area he spied a couple of Guardians pretending to read newspapers. They scanned the lobby every few moments, more concerned with spotting people trying to sneak *into* the hotel than anyone leaving it. But he knew the Guardians would stop him from venturing out, for his own protection. He had to get out unseen . . . *but how?*

A solution soon presented itself.

Sam spotted a passing waiter and fell into step behind him, changing his Stealth Suit to replicate the guy's black pants and white shirt, black tie and golden vest. They walked through into the kitchen area, where Sam ditched the waiter to head for daylight—a loading bay out back.

Peering around the corner, he saw a Guardian out in the alley, standing sentry. There was a truck pulled up with its rear cargo door open to the dock, collecting laundry. When the guy turned to load another big wheeled basket of dirty linen into the truck, Sam snuck into the next basket.

Eurgh! It stinks in here.

He shifted around on the load of damp towels and felt the basket being pushed across the loading bay, jarring hard as it bounced over the lip of the truck and then rolling smoothly over the metal surface inside. Sam held his breath against the smell and waited, silent, until he heard the clang of the truck doors slamming shut followed by the sound of the big diesel engine coming to life.

Sam waited until the truck had made a few short runs and stops before making his move. He crept out of the basket and made for the doors. The double-swing doors were sealed—*locked*—from the outside.

Oh man.

"OK, Jedi," Sam said, looking around the truck with the flashlight on his phone. "Didn't give me an app to get out of this, did you?"

Sam realized that the truck was not idling in traffic—its engine had stopped. The guy was at the doors, rattling the latches. Sam ducked back behind the big baskets of laundry.

Sunlight blazed in as the doors opened. Peeking through gaps between the baskets, Sam could see they were in an alley behind a restaurant, the truck driver walking through a doorway.

Sam slipped out the back and jumped down to the road, his Stealth Suit changing to the casual outfit he'd selected back at the hotel. Behind him, the guy loaded more laundry, oblivious to his recent traveling companion. Sam smiled, put on his sunglasses, then used the street signs and his phone's GPS to get his bearings. He headed for the Louvre, whistling as he walked quickly among the early evening crowd.

Who needs a Stealth Suit to be invisible . . .

ALEX

"This is the Enterprise's 'dream team,'" Shiva said with a grin. The big stainless steel doors, like a bank vault, closed behind them. "Have you been in here before?"

"Nup, this is cool . . ." Alex walked closely behind his friend, seeing Enterprise Agents all around them stationed at computers. But they weren't ordinary computers—each Agent had three huge screens. They all looked very young and seemed to be extremely focused. "They look like they should be working at one of those big-shot companies around here in Silicon Valley. You know, the ones where they're all on Segways and playing basketball at their desks."

"Them?" Shiva said, slowing so that Alex and he were walking shoulder to shoulder. "Please! Those Internet and social media guys are about ten years behind what we're doing here. Most of the tech Agents used to work for one of those companies or another—but we pay more, a lot more, and have the *real* cutting-edge tech here."

"Yeah, about that," Alex said, seeing Agents huddled around a wall of glass that was covered in pictures and graphics, like the world's biggest touch screen. They were manipulating images across the surface. "What are these guys doing?"

"Let's go see," Shiva said.

They walked over to the group. Alex could see that some images were pictures of cities, showing demonstrations and marches, disturbances taking place in the streets. The young Asian woman in charge looked at Shiva and smiled, then at Alex and frowned.

"It's OK, he's with me, a new recruit," Shiva said. "What are you working on?"

"We're tracking anomalies in the Dreamscape," the woman replied. "There've been mass protests and unrest in various spots around the globe, we believe as a result of a widespread nightmare epidemic. People are afraid they're being brainwashed in their sleep."

"You find a cause for it?" Shiva asked. "The source?"

"For the nightmares?" she said. "No. But this is unlike anything we've ever seen."

"It's because of the last 13, isn't it?" Alex said, seeing an image of Sam from a news report in the corner. "The race has changed the balance of things—in the dream world I mean."

"Yes, that's correct, though it does not explain things fully," the woman said, then she turned to the screen and wiped away some of the scenes of destruction and brought up what looked like a sine wave.

"This is how the dream wave for a normal night in a large city looks—for those asleep, there's a mixture of happy dreams, sad dreams, nightmares and so forth. The full mixture, and it's always in a proportion similar to this."

Alex and Shiva nodded.

"*This* is what we're seeing in these trouble spots as of last night," she continued.

The results were extraordinary.

"They're *all* having nightmares?" Alex said.

"What could cause that?" Shiva asked.

"We're not sure, that's what we're discussing right now," she replied. "We don't really have a frame of reference for this kind of rupture in the Dreamscape."

"That will do for today's lesson," a voice said behind Alex.

The group seemed to startle, and everyone hurried back to being busy and working elsewhere.

Alex and Shiva turned around.

Matrix stood before them, his hair pulled back into a long, greasy ponytail.

How did he know we were in here? That just good, or rather bad, timing?

"Matrix," Shiva said, "you remember Alex, our newest team member?"

Alex thrust out a hand, but Matrix kept his hands firmly clasped behind his back, his bulging stomach stretching his coffee-stained T-shirt.

"He doesn't like to touch other people," Shiva whispered out the corner of his mouth.

"Member of my team, huh?" Matrix said.

"Yes," Alex replied nervously.

"Well then, perhaps you should get back to work."

Matrix loomed in front of Alex's console back in the computer lab, staring blankly at him. Finally, his eyes narrowed and he stepped closer to Alex. "Until you earn it," Matrix said, his voice quick, "I don't trust you."

Yeah, right back at ya, buddy.

"Matrix," Shiva said, intervening. "Alex's good, he's been doing fine so far."

"I want to see what the kid can do," Matrix said, pointing at an old computer that had somehow materialized on Alex's desk. "Hack into the Academy's Swiss campus."

"OK," Alex said warily, before adding, "easy."

He switched it on. Nothing happened.

"I think you'll find," Shiva said, getting under the desk and coming out with a power cord, holding up the plug, "that you'll need to plug this in first."

"Yeah, I heard that helps," Alex laughed.

"I want you to isolate their communications systems," Matrix went on. "Phones, radio, all of it, get me access."

"Uh-huh," Alex said, his fingers drumming on the keyboard. "But why?"

"Why?" Matrix repeated, as though insulted that someone would question him. "Because I said so. Because it's a test. *That's* a five-year-old computer," he said, pointing to the dusty machine in front of Alex, "and *you're* a fifteen-year-old kid. Let's see what you can do. You have twenty-four hours."

"I'll do it in twelve," Alex said, his fingers already sending computer code flying up the screen.

Take that.

Matrix smiled, a thin smirk, then he turned and went over to his private, isolated corner of the lab.

Alex watched his back as he walked away. "I'll show him," he muttered, cracking his knuckles and turning back to his computer.

"Seriously though," Shiva said, "Matrix is hard-core. He works twelve-hour days here then makes a couple of million a year on the side through his own software business, not to mention his haul as a pro-gamer."

"What does he play?"

"Everything. He was world champ at *StarCraft* when he was seventeen. Practically rewrote the book on how to slay at *Guitar Hero*. Now, I don't know, I think it's like pretty much any game out there—he enters tournaments and collects titles, just for fun. He's a computer genius to the power of a million."

"Well, genius times a million or not," Alex said, opening up a new web browser, "the guy stinks. He may work and game all the time, but shower much?"

Shiva cracked up laughing so hard that tears started rolling down his cheeks. Alex stared, waiting for him to stop but Shiva just waved him away as he doubled over.

Sheesh, that's not even my best stuff. This guy's gotta get out more . . .

SAM

"If only I could walk through walls . . ." Sam said, looking in awe at the Louvre forecourt. The place was massive. And *busy*. Hundreds of tourists jostled one another as they headed for either the last hours of the museum's extended evening viewing or the sunset that was not far off on the Seine River. Summer storm clouds rumbled overhead. Sam walked fast, only to be caught up in the museum's entrance line.

He shuffled through the entrance in the large glass pyramid. With the Professor still tied up with his business at the Council, he felt he had the time to find Zara—to warn her, protect her. He bought a pass to join the day's final tour, and kept to the back of the group as they moved at a snail's pace.

On the way past the lines at the gift shops and food vendors, Sam felt several people stare at him.

What are they looking at?

It almost felt like he was in a dream. Then he remembered the news footage from Berlin.

Has some kind of local police report gone out for me?

Maybe there's been a reported sighting of me here, now that I'm a wanted fugitive.

There were a couple of cops ahead, casting an eye over the tour group, mainly made up of Americans, as it surged forward.

Sam stopped at the gift store and whizzed through the carousel of sun hats, selecting a cap with the Eiffel tower on the front of it.

By the time he'd paid and rejoined his group, the cops had moved on. No one seemed to be taking particular notice of him anymore. Everyone was too busy looking at the amazing artworks. He was back to being one of the faceless masses.

For now.

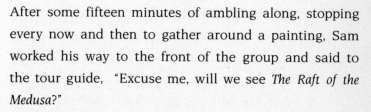

After some fifteen minutes of ambling along, stopping every now and then to gather around a painting, Sam worked his way to the front of the group and said to the tour guide, "Excuse me, will we see *The Raft of the Medusa*?"

"Ah, Gericault," the guide said, not breaking her stride. "No."

"No?"

"Different tour."

"Oh, OK. How about the *Mona Lisa*?" Sam said, latching

on to the name of the first famous painting he could think of.

"Yes," the guide replied.

"Cool."

The guide looked down her nose at him as they continued on. Sam drifted to the back of the pack, watching out for anything unusual.

The space around him was vaguely familiar, but in his nightmare he'd only seen the interior of the museum in darkness. They passed a couple of security guards and Sam looked the other way as he and his group entered another gallery.

The *Mona Lisa*.

The crowd in the room was like a mosh pit, a crush of people holding their cameras high overhead, trying to snap a picture of the little painting, some jumping to get a better view.

Wonder what da Vinci would make of this circus . . .

There was a wait for a few minutes as another group were shepherded away, continuing to take photos over the heads of those who now crammed in for a closer look. The guide spoke to them in a hushed tone, and Sam looked up—straight into the lens of a security camera above.

Oh no!

Heat flared up Sam's neck as he looked away.

Down the gallery, the security guards' radios crackled to life, and they both spoke into their handsets at once.

Quick, think!

Sam thought back to the dream, struggling to recall how he got from the galleries to the restoration room. He turned from his group, who were finally in front of the famous painting, and followed the other tour group out. All the while, he tried to get his bearings. As he did so, the two security guards entered the room—and he caught a few words of their conversation he recognized—*look out . . . teenager . . . red coat.*

Instinctively, Sam looked at the guy in front of him—wearing a dark-blue blazer over a T-shirt, and his Stealth Suit changed to mimic it.

A kid in the arms of a woman next to him started laughing and pointing at Sam's trick.

The laughing attracted the attention of the woman, who looked from the child to Sam, then back to the tour. She glanced back to Sam, as if something had registered.

Sam backed away.

Why is this bit always easier in the dreams?

The kid's older brother raised his hand to point at Sam.

Sam didn't wait to see what might happen next.

He turned and ran.

Down the length of the Denon Wing, its imposing arched ceiling towering above, Sam flashed by a cop, no doubt looking for a teen in a red coat. Sam rounded a corner, his shoes skidding on the floor, and checked back over his shoulder. The cop had doubled back, but by the time he'd come around the corner, Sam's Stealth Suit had changed again, this time into a tour guide's uniform.

He was no longer running, rather standing there and pointing down the hall.

"That way!" Sam said in just-passable French, and the cop blazed by without even looking at him.

A few minutes later, Sam was standing in the main courtyard outside. He was frustrated that he'd been unable to find the way to the room from his dream. The gendarmerie—the French police—were at the entrance to the museum, searching the crowd. He adjusted his sunglasses and cap, making sure he kept hidden among the masses of people. He was now dressed in casual clothes, typical of the young Parisians he saw around him.

Maybe the Professor was right—maybe I should have waited until tomorrow to meet Zara, to find another way.

But Sam couldn't shake the idea that he had to find her as fast as possible. The sun would soon set, and with it his chances of finding Zara would diminish.

If only she had a dream catcher necklace on, then I could find her on my phone.

Phone . . .

Sam pulled out his phone and dialed Jedi.

"Yo, waz up?" Jedi said.

"Any chance you can bring up the details we have on Zara?"

"You and the Professor trying to find her?"

"Yeah," Sam said. *Well, technically, it's not really a lie—we are trying to find her.*

"What kind of info you after?" Jedi said.

"Phone number."

"One sec . . ."

Sam could hear Jedi's hands tapping at the keyboard.

"OK, sending it to you now," Jedi said.

Sam saw the number flash up on his screen.

"Thanks."

"That it?" Jedi asked.

"Well, I was thinking," Sam said, wishing he'd thought

of it before, "if there's some way that you can track her location via her phone?"

There was a slight pause. "If she's on it, I can try, but I can't be sure how accurate the trace will be—I mean, I can try to piggyback the emergency network, but for an exact location it depends on her carrier and her position in relation to the telephone towers."

"Right, well, get ready to track her location; I'm going to call her now."

"All right then, let's do it."

Sam hung up. The problem was, if he called her and Jedi tracked her location to somewhere back *inside* the Louvre, that wouldn't really help. He assumed she was in there now, but there was no way he'd be able to get back inside to find her, not with all the guards now on high alert. He had to draw her out.

"Bonjour?" Zara said.

"Hi," Sam replied. "Zara?"

"Oui. Yes?"

"My name's Sam."

"And?"

"And . . ."

And what? I need to meet you, so I can tell you that you're part of the last 13 Dreamers who must take part in the most important race in history?

"How, ah," Sam said, "how are you doing?"

"Who is this?"

"Ahh . . ." Sam looked around, swallowed hard. "Zara, I need to talk to you about something important."

"Who *are* you?" she said, sounding annoyed.

"Sam."

"Where are you calling from? If this is a prank, I am hanging up now."

"I've come to Paris to meet you," Sam said, cringing at how lame this sounded. "I have information that you need to hear."

"Please explain. I don't understand. What information?"

"About who you are—"

"I am hanging up now, good-bye, Sam."

"No! Please, wait . . ." Sam said. He could hear her on the other end of the call, hesitating for a moment. He had an idea. "You're in the Louvre now, aren't you?"

"You're *following* me?" Her voice took on another, more urgent, tone.

"No. No, I promise. Look, there's a package there, in your restoration room, a postal pack, from a site in Italy."

There was silence on the other end of the phone.

"Zara?"

"Yes, it's here."

"It has images in it, of a lost da Vinci mural."

More silence.

"That package is still sealed," Zara said. "It arrived today."

"If you open it and see that what I say is true, you'll believe me?" Sam said. "Then you'll meet me?"

"I can't open it."

"Why not?"

"I'll lose my intern job. It is addressed to the head Renaissance curator, and she is not in until tomorrow."

It had already been opened in Sam's dream—which meant he was at least a day ahead. *A day ahead of Solaris, and everyone else, time which we have to make the most of!*

"Tomorrow, when it is opened, I will see if what you say is true. I have your number now, Sam, and I will call you."

"OK . . ."

"You can't just tell me what this important information is?" Zara said. "Is it—is it to do with the da Vinci?"

"It is, although not that one. If I told you over the phone, you wouldn't believe me."

"Then maybe we will speak tomorrow, and if it seems right, I will meet with you. In a public place." She hung up.

Sam paced. He wanted to maximize this small advantage he'd created.

The question came back into Sam's mind. Why *was* it always easier in the dream?

I was already there, with the next Dreamer, the introduction made or at least the setup in place.

He knew that once he changed what he'd seen in his dreams, such as being here now, contacting her, events would change—there'd be a ripple and the consequences were unknown.

Maybe there is a way . . .

Sam reasoned that if he could find the right vantage point, he'd have a chance of finding her in the crowd. He'd remembered about a student who was expelled from school after making a hoax call to the police—all because he wanted to get out of a math exam. He could still picture the kid getting marched out of class the next day by the grim-faced principal, towards his waiting parents who looked even grumpier.

Still, it did get him out of the exam.

This was no exam, and this wasn't a school.

But it just might get Zara out of the Louvre. And if I can use Jedi's phone tracking, I can find her.

Sam made the call to the police from a public phone in the nearby Metro station and walked back up to street level with an anxious knot in his stomach.

Well, I'm already a wanted fugitive, why stop now?

The outpouring of patrons and staff from the Louvre didn't take long to begin. In his call, he'd claimed that there were booby traps set at the fire escapes and other exits, loaded with stink gas that, although harmless, would make the patrons reek for days. He mumbled something about a protest against the decline of art. He hoped that it would mean that everyone in the museum would come out from within the glass pyramid.

Sam watched and waited. He stood on the stairs of the Richelieu Wing to the north, scanning the faces of the people streaming past. The fire alarm had been sounded and was a constant hum from the window behind him, soon pierced by the arrival of over a dozen emergency response vehicles.

A few heavily armed gendarmes ran past Sam, one of them looking at him a little too long. Sam disappeared around a column and changed his Stealth Suit to match the police uniform, then walked away.

His phone chimed. Jedi.

"Good news," Jedi said, his voice barely audible over the wailing of sirens and complaints of several thousand tourists. "Zara just made a call and the signal's strong enough to triangulate. I'm tracking her phone now."

"Cool, where is she?"

"Well, according to my screen, she's about fifty yards to the west of you."

Sam walked to the west, scanning the crowd as he moved, and spotted Zara walking quickly past the hastily erected security barricades.

"Thanks, got her."

"OK, but listen, be careful out there," Jedi said. "I heard

Zara's call—it was to her dad and she said there was a terrorist threat against the Louvre."

"Thanks for the heads-up, but I think I'll be fine," Sam said, ending the call. Once he'd rounded the corner, his Stealth Suit changed back to the casual jeans and hoodie that he preferred. Zara was a block ahead and he kept her within easy view, but staying back enough to blend in with the crowd.

Zara stopped outside the Sorbonne. Sam hung back and looked in a nearby window, watching her sideways through his sunglasses.

So this is where the Professor, Dr. Dark and the Enterprise guy met. Huh.

Thankfully, she didn't go inside. Instead, she was met out on the street by a man that Sam presumed must be her father.

He doesn't look like an Agent. Not at all like one of Stella's goons. Then again, it's those ones who are the best at the deception—living a fake life, never revealing their real intentions.

Sam forced the bitter thoughts from his mind and kept to the shady side of the street as he followed the two of them as they began walking together. They seemed happy.

Well, I'd been happy with my parents too, hadn't I?

All those birthdays, family vacations and movie nights.

And the times his parents had taken him to jujitsu and football practice.

Where are they now? Are they part of the Enterprise effort to track me down?

He checked his phone—thankfully there were no calls or messages from the Professor, which meant he was still at his meeting with the Council, or at least he'd not returned to the hotel to find Sam missing. No doubt when that happened, the Professor would ask Jedi to track Sam's location and would zoom in on him at once.

For my own protection, of course.

He'd only been with the Academy for a short time, but they already felt like his family now. The Professor, Lora, Eva, Gabriella and Pi, and hopefully even Alex, even if he was at the Enterprise—they were what mattered now. He had to push away the lie that his proxies had sold him his whole life.

Sam stopped and looked around. He'd been absent-mindedly thinking while walking and lost track of his targets . . . there, across the road, in a dark doorway. The streetlights blinked into life and he saw them clearly then. The Agent kissed Zara's cheek and they parted ways. The Agent went up into the apartment building and Zara continued down the street. Sam followed.

At the intersection she looked around, then turned a corner. Another street, another corner—

Zara was gone.

Sam doubled back along the Parisian street, looking at the passing faces in the fading light, searching for Zara. Fat drops of rain begin to fall and he took shelter under an awning for a moment.

He looked along the road and peered inside the cars passing by.

Where is she? Was she taken? Am I too late?

Sam was so lost in the terrifying possibilities of his failure that he almost missed her right in front of him. Zara was just inside a bookshop, directly across the street.

He crossed over and watched her from the edge of the large brass window that wrapped around the corner of the bookshop. Zara had her back to him, browsing between shelves crammed with books. He walked through the open doorway.

Inside the shop it was cheery, with music playing and people drinking wine at some soon-to-begin event where seats were arranged facing a table. Sam watched as Zara took a water and went on studying the shelves in the Young Adult section.

Sam took a glass of juice offered by a staffer and went to the next aisle, where he could see Zara between the open shelves. She had long eyelashes which flickered as she cast her eyes over the books. Her long, light-brown hair wisped across her face. As they both came to the end of the aisle, she suddenly looked up and stared directly at Sam, meeting his gaze with a steady look. Sam felt himself blush and turned away in a hurry. He picked up a book from the shelf next to him, *How to Win Friends and Influence People*, furiously trying to pretend he just happened to be there.

"Bonjour."

"Ah!" Sam dropped the book.

Zara picked it up, studied the cover, handed it back. She spoke quickly in French and Sam could only manage to catch a few words.

"I—ah . . ." Sam put the book back, upside down and back-to-front, and several books next to it fell to the floor as he leaned his elbow on the shelf. "I . . . ah, sorry, I don't speak much French. But if you hold on a moment, I have this."

He retrieved his phone and brought up the language translation app.

"Then it's lucky I speak fluent English," Zara said. She tilted her head slightly, studying him. "I'm Zara. But then, you may already know that?"

"I'm Sam." He put the phone away and picked up the dropped books.

"Sam? So, you phone me at work, then, what—then you follow me here?"

"Me?" Sam looked over his shoulder. "No. Of course not. Follow . . . why would I? It's just a coincidence is all."

"I'm not sure," she said, sipping her water, her gaze steady. "I thought you would know."

"Know? Ah, know what?"

"I thought you would know the reason for following me."

Sam swallowed and he was sure there was an audible little click in his throat. He drained his juice.

"I might just get a refill," he said, and headed down the aisle to get another glass, using the moment's distraction to gather his thoughts.

I've got to get it together. She thinks I'm some kind of stalker.

Zara continued to exude an air of calm, appearing not so much frightened as intrigued.

"So, what's going on here?" Sam motioned around—it seemed to be the time other shops around were shutting up for the day but this place was half full and getting busier.

"They do this every Friday, a little book soirée," Zara said flatly, unimpressed at his attempt at deflection and small talk. "Sam, it feels like I've seen you before."

"I have one of those familiar faces," he said.

Has she seen the news reports from Berlin too?

"Yes, very familiar . . ." she said. "Didn't I see you outside the Louvre just before?"

"Um, the Louvre . . . that's the museum, yeah?"

Zara nodded, not buying his dumb act.

"Hmm. Yeah, you know what," Sam nodded with feigned realization, "I *was* there today."

"Well, that *is* a coincidence," Zara said with a mock smile. "So was I."

"Oh, nice," Sam said, sipping his juice and hoping to hide behind his glass.

I'm not cut out for this kind of thing, I should just say it. "*You're not who you think you are and this life isn't what you know it to be. Zara, you're a Dreamer, one of thirteen people who must save the world.*"

Instead he said, "So, come here often?"

"Oh, là là! Please!"

"I mean, it's a nice idea, a book soirée," Sam said, looking at the crowd. "That's like a party, right?"

Zara didn't answer. She gave him a final measuring stare and promptly walked away.

Sam caught up with her outside.

"Zara, wait."

She turned around.

"What do you want with me, Sam?" she said.

"That's a long story. But it's important—vital—that you hear it."

She looked at her watch.

"Please, give me half an hour," Sam said. "Let's sit and talk someplace, I'll explain everything."

She paused, weighing up the situation.

"I promise you," Sam said, "that what I have to tell you will change your life."

She laughed despite herself. "Sam, you are either romantic, or crazy, or a schemer. Maybe all three."

"Just give me a chance to explain."

She looked up and down the street.

"OK, one chance," Zara said. "My favorite cafe is around the corner."

17

Ten minutes. Ten minutes of Sam talking nonstop and Zara had heard enough.

"OK, Sam," she said, finishing her espresso. "At least I now know what you are."

"A lonely hero trying to save the world?" Sam said, eating some of the almond cake he'd ordered while Zara's remained untouched.

"Non—you are a *crazy!*"

"A crazy?" Sam said, chewing. "Or, *or*, am I making so much sense that you can't handle it as the truth?"

"OK, listen carefully, Sam."

"Yes?" he said, giving her his full attention.

"You. Are. Absolutely. Nuts."

"We'll see . . ." Sam finished his cake and sipped his coffee. "You not hungry?"

Zara shook her head, silent for a while as they sat next to each other, looking out the window to the street outside.

"You *really* think you're telling the truth, don't you?" Zara said. Sam nodded. "A long-lost machine built by da Vinci, and a—a *dreaming* gene?"

Sam nodded.

"Which has been implanted in babies, hoping one day they can take part in a 'race' between good and evil, like a comic book . . ."

"The *ultimate* race," Sam said, half-jokingly, but his smile faded as he saw her expression. *She's mocking me, but then again, maybe she's starting to believe, just a little . . .*

Zara said, "Right."

"Yes."

"Yes?"

"Yes—that's what I believe," Sam said. "And you'll come to believe it too."

"You understand that it sounds crazy?" Zara said. "That you sound crazy. I mean, what, you're sixteen?"

"About that. Almost, nearly."

"Almost nearly sixteen. And you are the world's *only* hope?"

Sam nodded.

"You make this sound like some bad American movie, full of computer explosions."

"Exploding computers?" Sam said.

"No—with the computer-made explosions and fire and—"

"CGI, right. Anyway, look, Zara, I know I'm not very good at explaining this, and I know it sounds weird at first, but it's true." Sam pushed away his empty plate. "There will be thirteen Dreamers and like it or not, you're one of them.

I do know it sounds like I'm nuts. I was in your shoes just a couple of weeks ago. I didn't believe it either and it took me a while to change my mind, to believe."

"And what made you believe?"

"Things I've seen," Sam replied. "Things I've done."

"Like?"

Sam didn't quite know where to begin, so he reached under the neckline of his T-shirt and produced the golden key.

"What's that?" Zara asked, frown lines dimpling her forehead as she leaned forward for a better look.

"A very special key," Sam said. He passed it over. "It was inside a crystal sphere known as the Star of Egypt."

"This mark . . ." she looked up at him, her eyes wide-open in uncomprehending awe.

"Yes?" Sam said, smiling.

"I mean, it can't be . . . you know who this mark is by?"

"Da Vinci," Sam said. He fought the urge to say, "Ta-da!"

"*You* have his key . . . da Vinci's key. A key to what?"

"So far it has unlocked a secret box and it could also be the first part of his Bakhu machine. It points to a place—"

"It is for navigation?" Zara's eyes narrowed at this.

"Yes," Sam said.

She nodded.

Sam said, "It looks like that makes sense to you."

"It might . . ." she said, looking at the fine teeth at the end of the key. "My father would know. He's an expert on da Vinci, he could authenticate this. Maybe he knows of it."

"And then you'd believe me?"

It took her a while, but finally she nodded again.

"My father's not home," Zara said as she came back down from her family's upstairs apartment. "He must be out with my mother. They don't answer their phones."

Lucky break for me.

Sam couldn't work out how to tell her that her parents were Enterprise Agents.

Earn her trust first, then tell her that.

Outside Zara's apartment, they stood in the street, rain coming down in a fine mist. Zara shivered under an impossibly small umbrella. Sam felt dry in his waterproof Stealth Suit but the rain dripped from the edges of his Eiffel Tower cap and found its way down his exposed neck.

"That is a terrible hat," Zara said. "It makes you look even more American."

"I'm Canadian," he protested, adjusting his cap. "Well, technically a dual citizen."

"N'importe quoi . . . whatever. Come with me, I want to see if my papa is at his office."

"Ah, I'm not sure about that," Sam said, checking the time. The Professor had messaged Sam to advise he was coming back to the hotel. He was scheduled to return within half an hour. "How about we go via my hotel, and speak to the Professor first?" Then in answer to Zara's questioning look, he added, "He's the head of the Academy that I told you about."

And talking to "Papa" right now is not a good idea.

"Right, I see," Zara said.

"So you'll come?"

She shook her head, but Sam could tell that there was something there which had definitely shifted. She believed at least some of his story.

"I will meet you," Zara said. "You bring your Professor, and I'll talk to my papa about this key, about all this."

"Sure," Sam said looking around, scrambling for a way to delay Zara, or somehow convince her to keep a secret from her parents.

The storefront across the road was full of designer suits.

"Nice," Zara said, following his gaze. "Expensive, but worth every Euro."

"Yeah . . ."

Zara gasped and stepped back. Sam had changed his Stealth Suit to replicate the sleek black suit in the center of the display.

"*Pas possible!* That's—that's impossible!"

"For Dreamers like me, like us," Sam said with a smile, "a lot more than you think is possible."

Zara felt the sleeve of his suit jacket and said in wonder, "If I know how to do that, my wardrobe has just become a whole lot more affordable—and bigger!" She grinned.

"It's a type of memory fabric," Sam said. He changed his Stealth Suit back to his usual clothes. Then he changed to another suit in the window, a gray one. It reminded him too much of the Enterprise Agents, so he switched back to casual, but with a raincoat this time. He took off the tourist cap and flicked the hood up over his head.

"Tomorrow," Sam said. "I'll meet you at the Louvre?"

"Five—five o'clock . . ." Zara managed to say. "Meet me in the Denon Wing, at five."

"Any chance we can meet earlier?" Sam asked.

Zara shook her head. "Non. I have to work, it cannot be missed."

Maybe there are some things that just can't be changed, no matter how much you see into the future.

"OK, well, can you please do one thing for me?" Sam said carefully. "Don't tell your parents about all of this until after then. I want you to be sure, to really believe, then we can tell them together and I can answer any questions they may have."

Zara hesitated and nodded. "Anyway, I can't imagine what they would say about a stranger who says I have to help save the world!" she laughed.

Oh, I think you might find they'd believe you, Zara.

Sam stretched out his hand and she took it gingerly in hers. He gave her the tourist cap, and said, "Something to remember me by."

Sam took several wrong turns on his way back to the hotel and got back to his room with only five minutes to spare. He was drying his face and hair with a towel when there was a knock at his door. Through the peephole he could see the Professor standing there.

"Hey," Sam said, holding the door open.

"I brought you a treat," the Professor said as he entered the room.

Sam opened the paper bag—a couple of almond cakes.

Does he know where I was just now? Is he messing with me?

Sam marveled at the fact that he still knew so little about the Professor, *and* his abilities.

"Thanks," Sam said. "How'd your meeting go?"

"Good," the Professor replied, looking at the lights of Paris outside the darkening window. The top of the Eiffel Tower was visible, a blinking beacon against the night sky. "We're both going before the full Council at lunchtime tomorrow."

"Both of us?"

"They're eager to meet you, to hear what you have to

say," the Professor replied. He sank heavily into a chair. The day had clearly taken its toll.

"You seem worried," Sam said.

"When I met with the Leadership of the Council, I heard some disturbing news."

Sam waited for him to go on.

"Hans has control of the German Guardians, we knew that much already," the Professor said. "And now there's the possibility of serious division within the Enterprise."

"Division?" Sam asked. "You mean more than Stella?"

"Yes. Stella and her Agents, attacking you in Berlin, we're not sure if the director had any knowledge of it," the Professor said. "It's incomprehensible for them to use deadly force like that."

"As incomprehensible as the German Guardians turning?"

The Professor let out a deep sigh. "Sam, the Council Leadership is as confused as I am. The Enterprise is very powerful, with their cutting-edge technology and the huge number of Agents at their disposal, and those kinds of resources in the wrong hands . . . well, we are now waging a war on three fronts."

"Hans, Stella . . . and Solaris," Sam said. There was no forgetting him, that lone figure who kept to the shadows, driven to be the most powerful figure on Earth in his quest for the Dream Gate.

"That's right. Solaris we will work further on dealing

with," the Professor said. "It's the unknown extent of this Enterprise element that worries me most today. They know so much about us. Too much."

"I thought you knew this director guy, Jack—can't you talk to him?" Sam asked. "Weren't you friends before?"

"I wouldn't use the term 'friends,' but yes, we knew each other. And still do," the Professor said. He turned to Sam with solemn eyes. "I have spoken to him, tried to convince him that we should be working together against our common enemies." He sighed. "But Jack is very determined to do things his way. I cannot make him see that the last 13 is something we share. Something we need to protect."

Sam nodded. "Maybe we meet with Zara first tomorrow? Make sure she's safe?" he asked.

"Afterwards," the Professor said, shaking off his doldrums. "We'll make contact with her after our meeting at the Council. Thankfully her Agent parents will look out for her, and they may well be better informed about the movements of rogue Enterprise Agents than we are."

"Which means they only have Hans and Solaris to worry about," Sam said with a grimace.

"The good news is that only *we* know that she's the next Dreamer," the Professor said. "For now, she's just another Parisian teenager, albeit part of the Enterprise's Dreamer program. But there's dozens of them in the country, hundreds across the globe. So as long as no one else knows her true value in this race, she's safe."

Sam suddenly felt sick, worrying that by going to see Zara already he might have led anyone following him to her.

"We have friends in the Council who will support us, and our plans," the Professor was saying. "But it won't be simple. There are many differing views, especially with all the attention we're getting, what with the events in New York, Cairo, Rome and now Berlin . . ."

"Yeah, I know," Sam said, feeling the guilt about visiting Zara worsen. He fretted about the suspicion of the Louvre guards and police. "I've become a bit of a celebrity for all the wrong reasons."

The Professor seemed to be lost in thought for a moment. "I know it's hard, but try to get a good rest tonight because no matter what your dreams may bring, you're going to need it for what lies ahead."

ALEX

"Round two?"

Alex was waiting in a hallway for his mother to finish a meeting and turned to see Shiva grinning at him.

"Didn't I say tomorrow?" Alex replied. "And man, my legs are killing me from earlier!"

"Ha, well, just you wait until tomorrow—you'll hardly be able to walk."

"It'll be a fair fight then," Alex said grinning.

"You waiting for Phoebe?" Shiva said.

"Yep," Alex replied, "just going to grab some dinner together. You wanna come?"

"Thanks, Alex, but Matrix has us working 'round the clock now, twelve-hour shifts. I'm on my way back there."

"Bit of a slave driver, our boss," Alex laughed. "And what gives with the supersecret mission stuff?"

"I'll see if I can get you transferred onto this new project, amigo," Shiva said. "Then you'll know hard work." He winked. "I'd get booted out if I let you in even for a peek—we've gone hyper-max with the security."

"Seems everything around here's restricted," Alex said.

"I guess they have their security protocols for good reasons," Shiva said.

"Yeah, I'm sure," Alex said. "Look, Shiva, you wouldn't know where Sam is, would you?"

"Why would *I* know that?"

"Surely part of what you guys do is monitor everything that's going on in this race for the Dream Gate."

Shiva looked around like he didn't want to be overhead.

"You didn't hear this from me," Shiva said.

"I promise."

"Paris," Shiva said, walking away. "Your friend's in Paris . . ."

When Phoebe ducked out to tell Alex her meeting was running late, he began to wander the corridors, looking for something to occupy his time. He found himself outside the Agent training division.

Well, if I'm not allowed to play with the big boys in the computer lab, I might as well see what everyone else is doing.

In the first room, a handful of Agents were practicing at a pistol range with what looked like handguns, only they shot paint projectiles. Each time they hit the human silhouette down the range, a bright-blue splotch of paint exploded.

Alex walked past, smiling at the Agents and nodding

appreciatively at their target skills. "Keep up the good work!" he said, their faces stony in return.

With most Agents at dinner, the ops room was empty as Alex slipped quietly in. He ambled innocently over to a computer and casually clicked through the drives. A folder marked "SW' caught his eye.

What you got in there, Stella?

But when Alex tried to open it, an encryption lock appeared on the screen.

Oh, so you wanna play?

Alex's fingers flew across the keyboard as he tried to unlock the security on the file. Over and over "access denied' flashed on the screen.

"Argh! Come on, Alex, don't let her beat you," he muttered to himself. He looked across the silent room; there really was no one around. The perfect time for some spying.

"OK, what else can I try?" he said to himself.

Alex was absorbed by the challenge, minutes ticking by as he leaned closer and closer to the screen, until—

"Gotcha!" he punched the air as "access granted" pinged in front of him.

Alex scrolled through the files, opening some to find roster lists and reports on previous missions. One file was labelled "ACA OP."

This has today's date on it.

Alex double-clicked to open the file and stopped short

when he saw one particular entry—*Stella Wilde, forty Agents, on duty in Europe.*

"Stella's in Europe, again?" Alex said, then, making the connection, "And Sam's in Paris . . ."

He scrolled through the kit list and found nothing other than standard operating equipment. He was about to close the screens and return to the home page when he saw an update at the bottom of the file list. Stella had just picked up her vehicles in Austria.

"Austria?"

He clicked on the update. It included the payment of over a million dollars to a private security firm for the use of eight armed helicopters and flight crews for a twelve-hour mission.

"What on earth would you want all those armed helicopters for . . ?" Alex muttered, but before he could investigate further, he heard voices approaching and hastily shut the screen, racing from the room.

I need to talk to the director. Right now.

ZARA

Zara was wide awake late into the night. She'd heard her parents go to bed, waited an hour, then crept through the apartment to her parents' study. The walls were lined with bookshelves and she closed the door and flicked on a lamp. Inspecting the shelves, she took down as many books on da Vinci as she could find and spent two hours going through them.

Nothing. No mention of a special key, or a Bakhu machine.

But he did make machines of all kinds.

Who are you, Sam? And what is it you're really up to?

Yawning, she put all the books back, switched off the lamp and tiptoed down the hall to her bedroom. She climbed into her bed, pulled up the covers and closed her eyes.

ZARA'S NIGHTMARE

I am at work, I think. But it's dark and quiet. I'm meeting someone here but I cannot remember who or why. I walk through the rooms I know so well. I feel at ease in the presence of all this beauty, it makes me feel calm.

But something changes—there's a noise in the distance and then I turn a corner to see him. It's the boy from the bookshop but somehow I'm not surprised to see him here.

"Gericault's *The Raft of the Medusa*," I say as I walk up to him.

He turns to me as I stand beside him, then looks up at the impressive painting.

"A magnificent work," I add. "But not what you came for."

"Zara," he says.

I look at him. "Sam," I say.

We smile at each other.

"Follow me," I say. And he does. We are not in the Louvre anymore. We're not in Paris anymore. I smile, realizing I have been here before.

Da Vinci, of course.

We're walking through the house, creeping like thieves.

But we're not stealing, are we?

The fireplace is large and ornate. I reach out to touch it. It disappears at my fingertips, and before I can gasp, a lion is upon us, gone just as quickly, leaving us blinking in wonder at a whole new room.

This is not a dream—this is a hallucination.

Now I know I am far from reality. This place cannot exist. There are scrolls and books littered everywhere in the dusty workshop. My eyes struggle to make out objects scattered across the stone floor. Is this where the master worked? *Could it be?*

Sam is pulling at my arm, saying, "But for now we have to find what we came for."

I know he is right, so I go over to a creaky desk in the far corner. I rummage through the drawers and pull out a heavy box.

I am shivering and scared. We are swimming in freezing water, my clothes are dragging me down. It's dark, too dark. I can't see anything.

"Sam! Sam!" I shout. "Where are you?"

"I'm just here, don't worry," he says but my heart keeps pounding.

I cannot see him.

Why is it so dark?

Then I hear more splashes behind us. Shouts of men who are chasing us. I feel Sam grab my arm.

"Come on!" he whispers, "we can make it—"

"*Run!*" he shouts.

I chase after Sam, along the banks of the river, and look over my shoulder.

Men in gray suits are chasing us.

"They're Enterprise Agents!" Sam yells. "We can't let them catch us. Come on!"

Enterprise Agents? Like—like my parents?

I do a double take—I'm sure that one looks familiar, that he's a friend of my father's from the Sorbonne.

"Where are we going?" I ask—then I crash into the back of Sam. He's stopped abruptly and is standing stock-still.

Then I see the figures before us, a group of huge guys, emerging from the shadows.

"Who is it?" I ask, grabbing on to Sam's arm. My ears are ringing and my heartbeat thumps loudly in my chest.

"His name is Hans," Sam says.

There are at least a dozen men with him, huge and menacing. Our pursuers stop behind us, standing on the embankment, facing off.

We're trapped.

"You're out of luck, *boy!*"

That voice . . . it is terrifying. I can see that it freaks out Sam too. He's backing away a few paces from the sound of it, pushing us towards the river.

"Where do you think you're going?" the terrifying voice says. "You've got nowhere to run."

"This is Solaris," Sam says, and a figure steps forward.

I gasp as I take in a tall figure dressed all in black, shimmering as though in a heat wave. It's hard to focus on him. It makes my eyes hurt. A black mask covers his whole face. It's as if the darkness I hate so much has come to life.

Please, make this nightmare stop.

"And who's this?" Solaris says. "The next Dreamer, the next of the last 13? Ah . . . she *is!*"

"Leave us alone!" Sam shouts.

Solaris glowers and I feel my knees begin to give way from fear. I grip Sam's arm even more tightly.

The other two groups are standing still, as if frozen in time. The tension is unbearable—everyone is waiting to make their move.

Solaris says, "Tell me where they are . . . the key, the Gear . . ."

His voice, so deep and rasping, makes the hairs on the back of my neck stand to attention. I blink and suddenly Sam is choking, fighting to breathe. Solaris has him, and he is crushing his throat.

I cry out in horror, closing my eyes.

I must give him what he wants. I have to save Sam.

"Tick, tock," Solaris mocks, holding Sam off the ground by just one outstretched arm. His face is turning red. His arms claw uselessly at his neck, desperate for air.

"Let him go! *Please!*" I rush at Solaris. "What you want is in here!"

I throw Sam's backpack high into the air as I reach for

Sam. Solaris releases him, going for the backpack as I hoped he would.

But everyone else moves too, rushing at us, and just as quick–

There's an explosion of fire, a wall of heat and flames. I hear a mad, metallic-sounding laugh echoing loudly as I cling on to Sam. The fire is now everywhere around us.

"I gave you what you wanted!" I scream.

But there is only the heat now, smoke closing in on us, choking us. I look up to the night sky but it's all too late.

Beyond the flames, there is only the darkness that I dread.

SAM

Sam was flying, the wind pummeling his face, taking his breath away. Through the howling of the rushing air came another noise, an insistent ringing.

An alarm?

Again and again, louder and louder.

Ringing. A phone. Close by . . . *hunh?*

Sam came to and fumbled for the hotel phone sitting on the bedside table. "Hello?"

"Sam?" the Professor's deep voice said over the phone. "Are you OK?"

"Yeah, why?" Sam said, coughing and sitting up, the dream still pulling at the back of his mind.

Was I flying? Or falling?

"I thought you'd be down in the lobby by now," the Professor said.

"The lobby?" Sam swung his legs around and, carrying the phone, shot over to the window and parted the heavy curtains. It was bright daylight outside and the Parisian street below was abuzz with activity.

"It's eleven thirty, we must leave soon," the Professor said.

Eleven thirty!

"Right, I'm nearly ready, see you down there in a minute," Sam said, hanging up and hastily picking his Stealth Suit up from the floor.

His hair was sticking up in a mess and he tried to smooth it down as he ran down the corridor to the elevator.

I'm going to make a great first impression on the Council.

'Ah . . . now *this* is good coffee," Sam said to the Professor as they walked along, two Guardians up front and two behind. Sam adjusted his sunglasses in the late-morning sunshine and was pleased that no one seemed to recognize him today.

Hopefully some more exciting news has replaced my antics in Berlin by now.

Sam decided that he liked Paris. He admired the picture-perfect streets as the Professor prepped him for their meeting with the Council of Dreamers.

"How many Dreamers make up the Council?" Sam asked.

"Nearly two hundred, and they usually only meet once a year," the Professor replied.

"Always here?"

"No, but the Leadership meets here monthly—that's twelve men and women who have the overall authority for the Council's decisions."

"Twelve? Not thirteen?" Sam asked with a grin.

"Not everyone thinks that thirteen is such a lucky number," the Professor said.

"Oh. And you're part of the Leadership?"

"Yes, as I head the education programs at each of the Academy's campuses."

"Each? There's more than one?"

"The Swiss Alps and London campuses make up one quadrant." The Professor turned to him as they stopped at an intersection. "And the other three quadrants have a couple of campuses in their respective areas—over seven thousand students across eight countries."

The Professor looked at him sideways and said, "Sam, be prepared that many in the greater Council will be disbelieving of what you have to say, of what you've done. They may mock you, they will question your abilities, they might attack your credibility."

"I'll be OK . . ."

They crossed the road.

"There's one man, Mac, the deputy chairman, American . . . he can be hard to deal with, at times. He's quite vocal and he leads a group of Dream Gate skeptics."

"They don't believe it exists?"

"They see it as purely a legend, a myth that developed over the centuries. There have been false claims in the past, about searching and finding the Gate, and of the last 13. None of which turned out to be true, obviously."

"Until me."

"Until you. But there are those like Mac, who may believe in the mythology, but don't accept that it's actually a real, viable thing to discover."

"And what about da Vinci's Bakhu machine?"

"The wider Council will only learn about that today, hence the need for this special meeting and our appearance there. But some of them will think we're chasing ghosts."

"I'm sure I can handle this guy—Mac, was it?"

"Yes. But you only know the half of it," the Professor explained as they crossed in front of a Metro station and turned into another elegant street. "His group, about sixty or so of the Councillors, want you and the rest of the 13 used for other . . . *applications*."

"I don't like the sound of that."

"Hmmm. He'd like you all put to work, so to speak," the Professor explained as they crossed another tree-lined avenue. "Train you and the 13 to be able to steer your dreams, to better see the future, to prevent things from happening, like, say, another 9/11."

"Well, that doesn't sound like too bad an idea," Sam said.

"True, although I have seen other good Dreamers, how would you put it . . . go nuts," the Professor said. "They start out with good intentions, preventing crimes and atrocities, and then they get lost—they end up becoming addicted to steering dreams and succumb to the darkness that comes with that."

"Darkness?" Sam said.

They finally stopped at an intersection as traffic streamed by, all screeching tires and tooting horns.

"Predicting which stocks will rise tomorrow, which horse will win the next race, which political candidate to befriend because you know in thirty years' time that they will become President—that kind of power changes a person. I've seen it happen to the best people. Making millions of dollars then falling into power plays and political manipulations . . . it's a slippery slope."

Sam sighed.

This Dreamer stuff just keeps getting more complicated.

"Well," the Professor said, following the Guardians ahead. "Let's just wait and see where this Dreaming leads us." He turned to smile at Sam. "We're here."

"**T**his is it?" Sam asked as they entered a little restaurant. There were a few patrons, most of them sitting alone and eating lunch. The man closest to Sam was plucking garlic snails from their shells and slurping them down. Sam felt queasy just watching him. "I mean, I thought you'd have some kind of awesome meeting place, you know, like a palace or something."

"We are not quite there yet. This merely takes us to the tunnel," the Professor said. They walked through the dining room and into the kitchen. Pots and pans clattered and staff bustled around, all seemingly oblivious to the Professor and Sam and the four massive Guardians passing through their midst.

"Tunnel? To where?" Sam asked.

"There," the Professor said, pointing out a window to the rear alley. There was something poking out above the buildings at the end of the street, something familiar. "Is that awesome enough for you?"

"No *way!*" Sam said as he saw Paris' most famous landmark—the Eiffel Tower. A shudder ran through

Sam as he recalled a faint memory from his dream that morning.

Was I up there in my dream? Did I fall from the top?

"Way," the Professor replied with a chuckle. "Our Council headquarters are in an underground chamber that was once part of an old chalk mine, running right underneath the Eiffel Tower, which served as an early part of our operations."

"For what kind of operations?" Sam could hardly contain his curiosity.

"To keep track of dreams. As a giant antenna, if you will, to monitor the Dreamscape," the Professor explained as they walked down an ancient stone spiral staircase.

"You mean how people are dreaming, that kind of thing?" Sam asked.

"Yes, watching for any unusual changes in the Dream-scape, the types of dreams and so on."

"And you can monitor that globally?"

"To a degree. We can see many images of dreams which combine to show the bigger picture, so that we can gauge what kind of dreaming is going on. For over a hundred years the antennas were our main way of capturing trends in dreams around the world. Until Jedi brought his new technology online. He uses satellites and so on now."

"That's what he needs all the game consoles for? And all that power? That is *so cool*."

"It's one of the many functions Betsy serves. And yes,"

the Professor said, chuckling, "it is pretty cool. Now watch your step down here, the floor's a little slippery."

"This place looks really old," Sam said.

"Some of these mines date back hundreds of years," the Professor said. 'There are around two hundred miles of mine tunnels running under the city."

Sam looked around at the carved walls, the arching ceiling and the dark tunnels branching off into the gloom as they passed.

"Is this how the Council get in as well?" Sam asked, in his mind's eye imagining over a hundred guys like the Professor all shuffling along the same worn floor under his feet.

"Yes," the Professor said. "Although there are entrances and exits at each point of the compass. But everyone accesses the chambers via these tunnels, for safety and secrecy, of course."

They came to a heavy steel door, which the Guardians opened for them. Ahead was a vast cavern which stretched into darkness. As they walked further in, the way ahead became illuminated by LED strip lighting.

He could hear the Council before he could see it—the hum of a large number of people talking. Ahead, another huge steel door was set into the rock walls.

This is gonna be like talking in front of the whole school at assembly.

The Guardians stopped at the door, and held it open

for them to walk through. "That's as far as they go," the Professor said as he and Sam continued on. "The Council does not reveal its business to the outside world until it's ready."

"Not even to the Guardians?"

The Professor shook his head. They faced another door, this one smaller and modern, with a scanner which read the Professor's fingerprint. The door clicked open.

"Remember, Sam, don't worry if anyone doubts or questions you—just be honest and be yourself."

The Professor brought Sam into the Council's meeting room. There were eleven men and women at the front, seated at a raised table—the Council Leadership. The Professor took his seat among them. Over a hundred people were seated around in a tiered semicircular amphitheater, all looking down at him attentively, expectantly. Sam recognized several faces, business tycoons and politicians, a couple of sportspeople, prominent scientists, a member of a royal family and even a famous movie director. Dreamers and Council members, all of them.

Wow.

"Friends," the Professor's voice boomed from where he stood at a little wooden podium, the acoustics in the cavern such that the back row could hear a pin drop. "This is Sam. It is his dreams that are leading us to the rest of the last 13, and together, their dreams are enabling us to find that which the prophecy foretold."

Murmurs spread throughout the assembled crowd, echoing from the walls.

"Please," the chairman of the Council said, "let's hear the Professor out."

"Thank you—"

"*This* is our one, last hope?" a big guy with a bald head said. "This *boy?*"

Sam stood up a little straighter.

That's gotta be Mac.

"Come now, *Professor*, if this truly is the time for us to find the Dream Gate, it would not be left in the hands of a teenager."

"It's not the age of the *Dreamer* that matters, Mac, you know that," the Professor said. "It's the age of the *dreams.*"

Mac looked a little chastened then, Sam was pleased to see.

"Besides," the Professor said to all in the room, "Sam has proven himself, and more than once already."

"We've all seen the news reports from the Berlin Zoo," Mac said. "Not to mention the destruction in New York and Rome. Sam is too young and inexperienced for the task ahead—this is a job for skilled Dreamers with Guardians by their side."

"I'd like to point out," Sam said, stepping up to the

platform next to the Professor, "that none of that was me. Yes, I was there—but all the destruction, all those who have . . . not made it, that has been at the hands of others."

"Thank you, Sam," the chairman said. "For the assembly, can you tell us who those others are?"

"Hans and his rogue German Guardians," Sam said, "as well as Stella from the Enterprise, and of course, Solaris."

The uproar was both immense and unexpected. Sam took a step closer to the Professor for support.

Tough crowd. I can tell this isn't going to go well.

Those seated closest to Mac were shouting down Sam's comments, the rest of the Councillors joining in to argue in Sam's favor.

"Silence, *please*, silence!" the chairman said, rising to his feet. When the room finally quieted down, he sat back down. "We know that Sam has already come up against Solaris twice."

The murmur began again but this time it ebbed away quickly, followed by some whispers and glances.

"And the Enterprise?" a woman asked. "I cannot believe that they have done what is being reported."

"I'm afraid the evidence says otherwise," the Professor said. "You have all received my report on this. Two German Guardians were killed in the underground complex at the Berlin Zoo and they were killed by rogue Enterprise Agents. We are building further evidence of Stella's activities in Rome and New York."

"And if we're to believe all this," Mac said with a casual wave of the hand, "he's come out of those encounters with barely a scratch. How?"

The Professor looked to Sam to answer.

"Well, *I* survived," Sam said, "but others didn't. Among them, Sebastian and Tobias of the Academy." The nerves that usually overcame him when talking at the front of the class settled down, and he felt calm and collected. He made eye contact with many of those around him. He wanted to be sure they were listening.

Most faces looked sympathetic.

"And these 'Gears?'" the chairman asked. "Sam, can you tell us where you are at with locating all thirteen?"

"At the moment, we have one from Rome," Sam said, "and the key from inside the Star of Egypt."

"And Solaris?" the chairman continued.

"He—he has another Gear, taken from me in Berlin."

The chairman nodded. "And how many Dreamers have you found so far?"

Sam looked to the Professor for guidance but he just looked at Sam with trusting eyes.

"A few," Sam said carefully.

"A few?"

"The number is growing as I dream," Sam said.

Mac gave Sam a terse look and the chairman leaned forward.

"Sam," he said, "do you feel that you can continue to have these dreams?"

"I think so, yes," Sam said. "I'm only just learning about all this. It's all so . . . new."

"And do you feel confident in carrying on your mission to get the Gears?"

"For what it's worth," Sam said, "yes—I can do this."

The chairman nodded and turned to speak to a woman to his left as Mac whispered to those beside him.

"Sam," the woman asked, "how is it you have gone out on your own against Solaris?"

"Not always alone, ma'am," Sam replied. "Especially not at first, and it's happened by accident, it wasn't planned that way."

"We heard about New York," she said. "And Italy. But Germany—it was just you and another of the 13, another teen no less, up against Solaris, correct?"

"Yes," Sam said. "And the Enterprise and the German Guardians, trying to get Xavier and me. Xavier's father, Dr. Dark had been with us but he had to lead Hans and his—"

That drew the loudest response so far. Mac's people began shouting and pointing, which led to more arguing. It took a full five minutes for the chairman to be heard and for the din to die down.

"Please," the chairman said to the Council. "The Council cannot continue like this!"

Still, the room was not silent, with angry glances and murmured insults flying back and forth.

"We accept that there is a breakaway element of the Guardians, that is not in dispute," the chairman said. "And

Dr. Dark has verified it. It's only a pity that he could not attend this meeting to speak to the Council directly."

"The Enterprise—Agents of theirs, involved in a shoot-out?" Mac said, standing up and interrupting the chairman. "I'm not alone when I say that I find that *impossible* to believe. Impossible!"

"It was Stella," Sam said. "I know it was her because I—"

"This is ridiculous," another female Councillor said, her tone full of fury. "I move to suspend this meeting!"

Bickering swept through the ranks of Councillors until the Professor raised his arms for silence. Sam felt as though every face was turned his way and all were waiting for him to respond.

"OK," Sam said.

The silence that followed was eventually broken by the chairman, "Sam, what do you mean, 'OK?'"

"I mean," Sam said, "that some people will believe what they like. I've told you what I saw. I know who was there. If I'm not going to be believed, then that's the way it is."

"If I may . . . Mac, your reaction before intrigues me," the Professor said. "Do you care to expand on it, enlighten us?"

"No." Mac looked at the Professor.

"You see," the Professor continued, "Dark went to Hans, who he had assumed, being his old friend, would offer him safety—"

"Drop it, old man," Mac said, fire in his eyes.

"Well," the Professor said, not put off by Mac's rising

anger. "I'd like to, so I am sure we would all like to hear what it is you have to say about Hans. He was your business partner, after all . . ."

Mac stood up. He looked to those seated near him, who then rose in support. A few others scattered around the chamber stood also, including three of the twelve on the Leadership panel. Over forty people in total, Sam calculated.

"Chairman," Mac said. "Now that we seem to be at odds with what's happening and who is to blame, I believe this is an opportune moment to withdraw from the Council. I wish you all the best of luck in the coming race."

And with that, Mac led his followers from the chamber, leaving behind a stunned chairman with what was left of his Council. Sam looked to the Professor and saw that he looked both shocked and worried.

I guess he wasn't expecting that to happen.

24

"What now?" Sam asked the Professor, who had come down from the Leadership seats to sit with Sam.

"There's not been a split of the Council like this in my lifetime," he replied. "It shouldn't matter to us too much; things are moving so quickly now. The loss of some of the Councillors and their connections and abilities is disappointing, nonetheless."

Sam and the Professor watched as the Council regrouped. A lull had descended on the assembled Dreamers. The nine remaining in the Leadership rallied together and called upon three of the senior Councillors to step up and assume Leadership positions. Remarkably, no one seemed to object.

Looks like all the troublemakers just left. Maybe it'll get easier now . . .

"May I ask a question?" a Councillor to Sam's right said. He was a tall African man dressed in an impeccable white suit with a brilliant-blue tie. "What more have we learned about the Dream Gate? Our notes here before us are little more detailed than those we learned from when we were at the Academy as students ourselves."

Another member of the Leadership stood up to reply, discussing what little light had been shed, with a few more Councillors chiming in with their opinions.

"We're not ready for it!" one man said, standing so as to get attention and be heard. "The Egyptian Guardians are *right* when then say that we must be wary. The power beyond the Gate may be too much for humanity at the moment. Look at all the mistakes we still make, even here today in this very Council, full of so-called *enlightened minds*."

"*You* may not be ready," the African Councillor said. "But we are! The last 13 arising is proof of that, my friend."

Cheers rang out, but the argument continued back and forth, a few on each side of the fence, although the anger Sam had seen before with Mac was now gone.

"Looks like they'll be at this for a while," Sam said quietly to the Professor.

"A healthy debate, to be sure," the Professor conceded.

The discussion shifted to whether the ultimate power should be used, shared, hidden once more, or even destroyed.

I've been so busy just trying to work out where to go and what to do in this race, I haven't even considered these kinds of questions.

"If the Dream Gate leads to such a vast power, perhaps we're better off *never* finding it," an older woman at the back said.

"What are you suggesting?" the chairman asked.

"That we *don't* piece together this machine of da Vinci's," she replied. "That we hide the Gears as they come—that way, we control the race."

"And then have the Gate be lost forever?" the Professor interjected.

"Better lost than falling into the wrong hands," she replied. "We've survived well enough without this treasure."

"Survived? We could *thrive!*" the African Councillor said loudly. "This is our chance to reach our full potential."

The argument rumbled on and Sam found it hard to stay focused on the discussion.

They can talk all they want. I've gotta get out of here and do something. We have to get to Zara.

"Don't these people realize the race is going on out there, right now?" Sam whispered to the Professor. "The time for talking is over."

"They'll come around, Sam," the Professor said. "I'm afraid it's going to be a long day, and this Council needs all the voices of reason available. What do you think about leaving and trying to make contact with Zara?"

"On my own?"

"I need to make sure we're all in this together. We need the Council and their global influence to stand a chance."

"Well, sure," Sam said, checking his watch. "I'll meet Zara, leave it to me."

"You, and some Guardians to watch out for you."

Sam hesitated. "You're sure they're OK?"

"Larry and Harry, the two who stood guard outside your room this morning," the Professor said. "I've known them since they were your age. You can trust them."

"OK, thanks," Sam said. "So what should I do?"

"Get Jedi to help you find Zara. Then bring her with you to the hotel. Hopefully she's had her dream about the next Gear. If not, it won't be too far away."

The Professor squeezed Sam's shoulder. "I believe in you, Sam."

Sam smiled and slipped out of the Council room, happy to leave the arguments to the so-called grown-ups.

Larry and Harry were waiting outside the second door. They must have been advised of the new plan by the Professor, as they escorted Sam out of the tunnel and into the bright afternoon outside the cafe without hesitation.

"Where are we headed?" Larry asked.

"The Louvre, Harry."

"I'm Larry."

"Right," Sam said, eyeing the two hulking guys striding along beside him. "I was just saying, let's go to the Louvre."

Sam's phone beeped. It was Zara.

Sam—change of plans, meet me at the bookshop. Hurry.

"Or not . . ." Sam said.

"What is it?" Harry asked.

"Change of plans, Larry."

"I'm—"

"Just try and keep up with me!" Sam said, taking off at a sprint.

"I'm glad you called," Sam said as he and Zara sat by the window of the cafe near the bookstore. "I worried that you might not. How did you get out of work early?"

"I couldn't concentrate on what I was doing," Zara said. "Everything you told me last night, it's buzzing in my head. I could hardly sleep. But then . . . I had a dream."

Zara told Sam what she could remember, then paused, adding, "When I fell back asleep, I saw more—we met at the Louvre, at five o'clock, as planned. But the man was there, in black clothes, who chased us—shooting fire at us. The whole of the Denon Wing burned to the ground. But then I saw him somewhere else. It does not make sense, does it?"

Sam swallowed hard.

If that was due to happen at the same time I was supposed to meet her—five o'clock today, then Solaris is probably already in Paris.

Sam instinctively looked outside at the two Guardians, Larry and Harry, standing on constant alert. He felt a little better.

"So now you know why I wanted to meet earlier," Zara

said. "I wanted to change something. I couldn't let that happen. I'm right, non? That was one version of the future?"

"Yes, you're right. I'm glad you trusted your instincts," Sam said. "Does the dream mean something to you? Do you know where we have to go?"

"It was strange," she said. "After the fire, it's like I—how do you say, faint?"

"Fainted," Sam said, "like, you blacked out?"

"Oui, yes. And in the dark I was scared . . ."

Sam could see in her expression that recalling the dream was still terrifying to her.

"But I did see something else. Not at first, but this morning, when I looked through my father's da Vinci books again, it brought back a memory from my dream."

"Oh?"

"I'm sure I was at the manor house Clos Lucé where da Vinci had his last workshop. He spent the last three years of his life there. It is a museum now."

Sam's face lit up. "Could the Gear be there?"

Zara smiled. "It *is* there—I believe I have seen it!"

"Seriously?" Sam said, sitting up, his heart rate going crazy. "It's at the workshop?"

"But not in plain sight. In the dream, it is hidden, in a secret room. I thought my mind is playing tricks on me, but slowly I realize maybe it's not so crazy. It feels so *right*." She shrugged. "I cannot explain it."

"No explanation necessary, trust me. We need to get

there," Sam said. "How far away is it?"

"A few hours' drive," she said. "My papa can take us."

"Your father, right . . ." Sam looked out the window, absently, wondering how to tell Zara what he knew about her parents.

Zara, the people you love, who raised you—they may not actually be your parents.

"Maybe it's best you leave them out of this," Sam began.

"I can at least tell them where I am going, non?"

"Well . . ." Sam said.

Maybe that dart first and explain later technique of Sebastian's wasn't so bad after all.

"What do you think of your parents?"

"Think? I do not understand," she said.

"You know . . . do you like them?" Sam tried.

"Of course."

"Right, erm . . ." Sam gazed out the window. "Why don't I introduce you to the Professor first?"

"*Now?*" Zara said. "Look, Sam, I believe you, right? You told me about all this da Vinci dream stuff yesterday, then—then you change your clothes right in front of me. I dream of some secret da Vinci Gear, of an evil man called Solaris, just as you said I would. So what now? If we wait, maybe Solaris gets to us before we can get to the Gear?"

"When you put it like that . . ."

"My parents are so close now, and you have the protection of those two thick-necked guys out there."

"You know they're with me?"

"A little obvious, and I have seen bodyguards before at VIP events at the Louvre—they have a look about them."

Sam had to admit, Harry and Larry certainly stood out.

"So," Zara said, standing to leave. "How are we doing this?"

As they opened the door to Zara's apartment, Sam felt sick to his stomach.

We shouldn't have come here . . .

Furniture was overturned, drawers were emptied all over the floor, the cupboards were open, papers were scattered everywhere.

"Wait here," Harry said, moving past Sam and into the apartment, dart gun in his hand. Larry stayed in the entryway with Sam and Zara, who seemed frozen in the moment, shocked.

"My mother . . ." Zara said. "She was here this afternoon."

"Place is empty," Harry said, coming back to the entryway. "Every room's been turned over."

"What were they looking for?" Zara said.

"You," Sam said. He turned to her. "They were looking for you."

"*Me?*" Zara said, tears in her eyes.

The Sorbonne was busy, hundreds of students leaving as afternoon classes finished.

"I will go check—"

"Zara, wait!" Sam said, chasing after her and pulling at her arm. Zara turned around. Worry was etched on her face. Neither of her parents were answering their phones. "Let's go together, the four of us, OK? Stick with us, just to be safe."

She looked from him to Larry and Harry. "OK, but we run!"

The four of them ran inside, down a corridor that twisted and turned and then up two flight of stairs to the second level.

"It's up here," Zara said, panting.

"This one?" Sam asked, pausing by a door.

Zara nodded, getting her breath back.

Sam gave Harry a nod, and the huge Guardian took the command. He went through the door, dart gun drawn.

"It's OK guys, come in," Harry called.

Sam and Zara went inside the classroom, while Larry

stood guard in the hall outside.

"Papa!" Zara ran to her father and the two embraced. "I went home, someone has—"

"I know," her father said. "Your mother just called me, she's home now, packing some things and will meet us out of town. I'm sorry I missed your calls. I didn't mean to worry you."

"She's OK?" Zara was relieved.

"Yes," he said. "She came back to find the apartment had been broken into."

He looked at Sam and Harry.

"Papa, this is my friend, Sam," Zara said.

Sam could see recognition flit across the man's eyes. He also saw kindness, and someone who seemed trustworthy, Agent or not. Zara's father came over and shook Sam's hand. "So, *you* are the one," he said.

"That's what they tell me," Sam replied.

"And Zara?" he asked.

Sam nodded, said, "She's special too."

Zara's father beamed a smile. When he looked back at his daughter, she had confusion in her eyes.

"Darling," he said, "there's something that I must tell you."

"Papa?" Zara said, tears in her eyes.

"It is true."

"Which part?" she asked. "That I'm created? That I'm a Dreamer? That you are . . . you are not my father?"

Sam watched her tears fall as the man's silence confirmed most of it, but then he said, "You are our daughter. It is—we were part of a program, having you."

"Why?"

"To see if we could raise a powerful Dreamer."

"You've lied to me my whole life!"

"Zara, please . . ."

Sam paced the room, uncomfortable to be witnessing this conversation again.

This is just as terrible as when Xavier had this fight with Dr. Dark.

Zara banged her hand down on the table.

"For what?" she said. "So that you could raise me until my dream and then hand me over to the—the Enterprise when I started having these dreams?"

"What dreams have you had?" Mr. Armand said.

Zara looked to Sam, uncertain whether to say more.

"It started with my dream," Sam said. "My dream led me here. It leads me to the others when they are ready."

"Ah, *that's* why you are the one," Mr. Armand said. "Yes, you are the key, the one who will bring them together, to get to the Gate. And this is a Guardian, of course."

"I'll be waiting outside, but we shouldn't stay here for long," Harry said, leaving the three of them there.

"He's right, we should keep moving," Sam said. "But first I have to ask . . . Mr. Armand, are you with us or against us?"

Zara flashed an angry look at Sam. "What are you saying?" she demanded.

"Non, ma cherie, Sam is right to be suspicious," Mr. Armand soothed. "He knows the Academy and the Enterprise have not had the same agenda." He turned to Sam, came close to him. "But I promise you this, Sam. I will never allow harm to come to my daughter and I see now that the Academy wants nothing but to protect her. And there are others who might seek to hurt her."

"So you won't call it in?" Sam insisted.

"Non. The prophecy of the last 13 is more important than any loyalty to an employer. I think the time has come for all of us to make Signore da Vinci proud."

As Mr. Armand's phone chimed, Harry rapped his knuckles on the open door frame and motioned to Sam that they should go.

Zara's dad had answered the call, speaking quietly for a moment before hanging up.

"Your mother is headed out of town," he said to Zara. "She noticed that she was being followed, so she's leading them out on a scenic drive to Normandy."

"We must leave," Zara said. "We should help her."

"Your mother has been trained for situations such as these. I know that's hard to imagine, but she is stronger than you think," her father said to her. "Your job is to help Sam now."

"I'm sorry, Zara, but he's right," Sam said. "We should go to the Professor, then to da Vinci's workshop."

Zara quickly told her father about her dream.

"Through the fireplace . . ." he said, his eyes distant, picturing the adventure ahead, the possibility of discovering a secret room of da Vinci's not seen since it was sealed up and lost to history. The afternoon sunlight was now so low it beamed in through the open curtains and he went to the window to close the blinds.

"You shouldn't be here . . ." Mr. Armand went on. "It's too dangerous, there's so much at stake. Your lives are too important. Go now."

"But Papa—"

"No," Mr. Armand said, turning around. "Right now, you are two of the most wanted people on the planet. There are enemies that will stop at nothing to get at you. Please, go now. I'll stay here and make a distraction should anyone be following me to find you."

"Papa, I think you are overreacting a little, non?"

"No," he said, looking out the window and down at the street. "Look here."

Down in the leafy avenue, two SUVs had pulled up at the curb and burly men were piling out of every door.

"Who are they?" Zara asked. She pulled away from the window, startled.

"Not friends," Mr. Armand replied.

"Hans," Sam said, recognizing him. "And the German Guardians."

"Traitors . . ." Larry said, appearing by Sam's side and looking down to the street.

Mr. Armand went to his desk, opened a drawer and flicked a switch. Behind him, the blackboard slid up, a shiny steel panel behind it folding open to reveal an assortment of weapons.

Sam and Zara just stared, stunned.

We are way out of our league.

"Go meet up with Sam's people," Mr. Armand said, clipping a canister of tear gas into a grenade launcher. "Be safe with them and meet your mother near Clos Lucé. She can help you at the da Vinci workshop and then take you someplace safe."

"What about you?" Zara said, her voice wavering.

"I'll hold them off here." He passed Sam a couple of stun grenades.

"But you might . . ." Zara pleaded in vain.

"Never forget I love you. Now, go," Mr. Armand said, hugging his daughter and then pushing her away. "Take the stairs to the roof and run across to the west wing. Go down to the street from there."

"Papa?"

"Go!"

"Harry, Larry," Sam said, "stay here with Zara's father."

"We have to protect you," Harry said in protest.

"And if you hold off Hans' guys here, then you *are* protecting us," Sam said. He turned to Zara's dad. "No offense, Mr. Armand, but even with all this," he waved his arms at the weapons behind him, "you don't stand a chance here alone."

Mr. Armand nodded.

"And Hans' guys will think we're still here because you two are here," Sam said to Larry and Harry. "Zara and I will slip out and go to the Council headquarters; you know we'll be safe there. And besides, you two know better than anyone how to deal with Hans' team of Guardians."

Harry and Larry shared a look—they could see the reasoning in the plan. The German Guardians had left the street below. They were now somewhere inside the building.

"Good luck, my man," Harry said, shaking Sam's hand.

Zara placed a final kiss on her father's cheek. Sam took her hand, and they fled the room to the sound of the three men locking and loading.

ALEX

Alex and Phoebe swung into step with the director as he was power walking through the park outside the Enterprise HQ.

"What is it?" the director said, stopping in his tracks at seeing the panic on their faces.

"We've got news," Alex said.

"Oh?" the director said.

"It's about Stella," Alex said. He paused, looking for a reaction.

"I'm listening." The director waited for him to continue. He gave them his full attention.

"Well . . ." Now that the time had finally arrived, Alex wasn't sure where to start.

"Stella's turned, Jack," Phoebe said. "She's a double agent. She's got other interests aside from working for us."

The director stared at them both. The sweat from the humid morning beaded on his forehead, which he wiped away with a handkerchief.

"What do you know about it?" the director said.

Phoebe brought him up to speed with what they knew,

but when she finished the director merely frowned and remained silent.

"Well?" Alex said. "Haven't you got anything to say about it?" He ignored his mother's hand pressing on his arm. "She could have killed Sam in Berlin, and other people *did* die. And she's in league with *Solaris*? Are you *hearing* us?"

"That's enough, Alex. Let Jack speak," Phoebe reasoned.

I know he's her boss, but come on! What's wrong with him? Why isn't he ordering Stella's arrest or something?

"I didn't realize the scale of it, I see that now . . ." the director said. "I underestimated how much she'd done and—"

"Whoa! Hang on. Are you saying you already *knew* Stella was working for Solaris?" Alex's voice carried loudly across the park.

"Who do you think you're speaking to?" the director growled. "And lower your voice. It's hardly in our best interests to advertise this situation to anyone who walks by."

"Alex, calm down," Phoebe cautioned, then rounded on the director in a frantic whisper. "But how *could* you?" "Lives are at stake here, the *world* is at stake."

"I am fully aware of that, Agent Robertson," he said. "Now, will you both allow me to explain?" He ran his hand through his graying hair and took a deep breath. "I'd been warned about something like this. From the Professor. I didn't want to believe it at first . . ."

"It's true," Alex said. "She's a traitor."

"I agree, but I knew she couldn't be working alone, so I've been watching her—had others watch her—waiting to find out who she was working with, to find out what her objective was. I thought we had it under control."

"Who was spying on her?" Alex asked.

"Someone I believed could find out anything about anyone," Jack said.

"Matrix." Alex grimaced.

The director nodded and said, "I don't know how he could have missed all of this."

"Unless . . ." Phoebe began.

"Matrix isn't on our side anymore," Alex finished.

"Phoebe, grab your closest Agents, find him and shut him down!" Jack said. "Trust no one but your most loyal. Who knows how many Agents she's already turned."

All three of them began running across the park, heading straight for the Enterprise building.

"There's one more thing," Alex gasped as he kept stride with the director. "Stella hired a fleet of attack helicopters in Austria. Where would she be going with them?"

"Austria?" the director said, his eyes wide with terror. "That's within range of the Academy's Swiss campus . . ."

That realization hit Alex in the gut, hard, and spurred him on.

EVA

Eva walked into the corridor from her history class and bumped straight into Pi coming in the other direction.

"Hey, Pi," Eva said.

"Hi, Eva," Pi said.

"What'd you just have?"

"Literature," he said. "My favorite."

Students rushed by as they headed to the day's final classes. The two of them walked in the direction of the common rooms.

"I never did ask, where are you from?" Eva said.

"It's not obvious?" Pi said with a grin. "I'm an I-I."

"A what?" she asked, puzzled.

"Irish Indian." Pi laughed at Eva's surprised face. "My dad was born in India and went to the Academy in London, and met my mom there. She's Irish. They moved back to Dublin, had my brother, who's a Guardian now, then me and my kid sister. They've sent me here for the first couple of junior years."

"So you'll go to the London campus for your senior years?"

Pi nodded.

Gabriella and Xavier joined them.

"Where are you going now?" Gabriella asked.

"I've got gym class," Pi sighed. "*Not* my favorite."

"Library study, like you guys," Eva said.

"I've got a much better idea," Xavier smiled. "Come on, follow me."

Eva tried protesting but she had to run to keep up with Xavier, with Gabriella and Pi close behind. He led them outside the main building of the old monastery to a balcony on the cliff edge.

"Where are you *going*?" Eva asked as Xavier lifted a leg to get over the stone railing.

"Someplace cool, come on," he said. He turned to face outwards—then he stepped off.

"XAVIER!" Eva rushed to the edge, reaching out, too late.

"It's OK!" his voice called up from below. "Come check it out!"

Eva peered over the edge and saw that Xavier was about six feet below, standing on a snow-swept platform.

"Xavier!" Eva yelled at him. "You gave me a heart attack, you lunatic!"

Then just like that, he disappeared.

"Wha-at?" Eva gasped.

Gabriella was already over the handrail. "What are you waiting for, Eva? Scared, are you?" she taunted as she jumped off. "Oh, *wow!*" she cried out, disappearing from sight.

Scared? As if!

"What's down there?" Eva said. "Guys?"

Pi climbed over and took a deep breath. He shrugged at Eva and said, "Has to beat gym class."

"Pi, you don't have to—"

He dropped down.

"—go." Eva peered over the edge to see Pi had landed in a mess but dusted the powder snow off his knees and got up.

"Awesome!" Then he too vanished.

"Great," Eva said, climbing over the balustrade and then to the ledge, holding on to it by her hands until—

Drop.

THUMP.

Eva got up and saw that the other three were taking turns to slide down an icefall, so slick it looked like a clear glass water slide. It ended a few yards below in soft snow.

"Come on, Eva," Gabriella said, out of breath and laughing as she clambered back to the top of the slide. "Don't be a baby!"

"I don't really—"

Gabriella gave her a push.

"Arghhhh!"

Her landing wasn't graceful, but the snow was soft fresh powder, blown onto this flat rock shelf by the winds, and it was *fun*.

When was the last time I really had fun?

Pi landed next to her in a splash of snow. Eva took another turn and then another. Taking a break, she stood at the bottom of the slide while the others continued to collapse in giggling heaps, their shrieks echoing across the white valley below. She looked across to the mountain opposite, to where she'd trekked a few days before.

But why would Tobias be out there? Why would anyone *be out there?*

Gabriella landed next to her and got up, peering out in the same direction.

"What can you see?" Gabriella said, "Something is there?"

"I'm just thinking," Eva replied tensely, edging away from her.

"No," Gabriella said, pointing. "There *is* something, beyond the mountains. Si?"

Eva saw several tiny dots in the air.

Birds?

They were slowly getting closer and closer. And they were headed straight for the Academy.

Those aren't birds . . . those are helicopters.

SAM

Zara had tears in her eyes as Sam led her from the room. Before the doors to the fire stairs closed behind them, Sam heard the commotion of Hans' team moving in and the bang-cough of several tear gas grenades being launched in defense.

Did they track me here? Did they follow me?

"This way," Zara said, taking the lead. They took the steel fire stairs all the way down to street level. "Do you know how to get to the Council chambers?"

Sam retrieved his phone and opened the map app—it wasn't working.

"My message didn't even get through to Jedi," Sam said.

"Where was the Council meeting place?" Zara asked.

"Um . . ." He couldn't remember. He looked around to get his bearings and saw the top of the Eiffel Tower.

Sam used Zara's phone to locate the hotel, and then the Tower as a point of reference, figuring on following the route he'd walked with the Professor that morning. As they ran, they heard the pitter-patter sound of gunfire from the Sorbonne, streams of police vehicles rushing by.

Sam found the disguised restaurant entrance to the Council half an hour later. By the time they were underground at the first steel door, he knew something was wrong.

"Oh no . . ."

"What is it?" Zara said, waiting to continue as Sam stopped. "The door's open, let's go."

"There are no Guardians here," Sam said. By the dim lights of the LED strips lining the floor and ceiling corners, he could make out dark stains on the ground, slick and wet. He knelt down and touched it. It was red, and felt sticky and still warm.

Blood.

"Maybe we should turn back?" Zara said.

"No," Sam said, standing up and peering through the doorway. "I have to see."

"It's empty," Zara said.

The Council chamber was deserted. There was no one to be seen. Sam was explaining to Zara what the place was when there was a loud *BOOM!* and then a long rumbling noise from the direction they'd come.

"The tunnel!"

Sam ran to the first steel door—beyond it was a solid mass of rubble.

"Someone set an explosion, sealing off the entrance," Sam said. The lights flickered a few times, a couple exploding in a shower of sparks, and then they stayed off.

"There are other ways out," Sam said, remembering what the Professor said about the exits at each point of the compass. He switched on his phone's night vision app. "Follow me, stay close."

"What if they're blown up too?" Zara said, her hand on Sam's shoulder as they navigated in the darkness. "Or if we're in them when . . ?"

"Good point." Sam paused and looked around the room. "Wait here a second."

Sam moved off, leaving Zara to stand there in the gloom as he explored.

"My phone light doesn't work. Sam? Sam—did you hear me? Sam? Where are you?"

"Up here," Sam said, lighting the way for her. He was behind the Council Leadership table, standing at an open door. "I think I've found our way out!"

Above the Council chamber was a series of rooms that resembled Jedi's computer lab, only this had equipment that looked about as ancient as the old NASA control boards Sam had seen once in a documentary about the space race.

"What is all this stuff?" Zara asked as they searched around.

"Something to do with tracking dreams, or, like, reading the global trends of dreams, or something."

"And you think this is a way out?"

"Yep." Sam found a steel-rung ladder set into a vertical concrete shaft. Sam craned his neck to see the way out at the top. "I hope you're ready for a long climb." He set his foot on the bottom rung.

Here goes nothing.

Eventually, they came to a concrete platform, lit by one small grimy light, where the ladder switched sides.

"Sam," Zara said, catching her breath as Sam stopped for a rest. "What do you think happened to all the people who were meant to be back there?"

"I don't know," he said. "But there wasn't that much blood, and there were no bodies. So I'm thinking whatever went down, it could have been a lot worse."

Zara nodded and looked up at the ladder still stretching far above them. "Do you know where this is headed?"

"Yeah," Sam said. "I think I have an idea."

Sam opened a door into what looked like a big engine room, lit by more dirty lights.

"And we are under . . ." Zara began.

Sam didn't answer her. He went through another door and straight into a museum. It was full of old elevators and pictures of the Eiffel Tower through the years. Tourists turned in surprise to see them coming out of a staff exit.

"La Tour Eiffel," Zara said.

"The Council was once plugged into the Tower as some kind of antenna," Sam said.

They exited out of the basement level of one of the four legs of the massive steel structure and into a swirling sea of tourists. Above them towered the most famous landmark in France. Sam looked around for the quickest way up.

"Still no word from my papa," Zara said checking her phone.

"He'll be OK," Sam said. "Come on, let's move."

"Where to?"

Sam took Zara by the arm and jumped the line, ignoring howls of protest. He dived straight into one of the elevators, pulling Zara in behind him as the doors shut.

Outside the elevator, a new scene greeted them.

Hans. He and four of his German Guardians came running towards them, scattering unsuspecting tourists as they ran, trying to reach Sam and Zara.

Then, Sam saw something else. As the elevator car rose to the first platform, Sam got the slightest glimpse, of a tall masked figure in black, moving towards another of the Tower's legs.

Solaris.

Where do we hide from him *on the Eiffel Tower?*

"**M**y phone's still got no signal," Sam said. "Let me try yours."

In the rising elevator in the Eiffel Tower, Zara passed her phone to Sam. He punched in Jedi's number and the call was answered immediately.

"Yes!" Sam said, but then his heart sank.

"Hey, you've reached Jedi, I'm saving the world from evil forces right now so leave a message after the tone . . ."

Voice mail? Man, not now!

"Jedi! It's Sam, look, my phone's out so call me back at this number, it's Zara's. We're in Paris and the Council was attacked. It could have been Hans, he's here with the German Guardians. Right now we're at the Eiffel Tower and Solaris is—"

"Sam?"

"Jedi!" Sam was elated to hear his voice break in.

"I let the computer screen my calls," Jedi said. "I just heard from the Professor."

"He's OK?" Sam interrupted.

"Yes, but there's been a cyber attack against us, and all

our phone networks worldwide are being jammed," Jedi said. "Not that it stopped me for long, but I think just about everyone else is offline for now. I'm working on it, though."

"Jammed?" Sam asked.

"It must be Matrix," Jedi said. "Which means the Enterprise are making a move."

"We're going up the Eiffel Tower right now." Sam watched as they soared higher in the elevator, the milling Parisians below getting ever tinier. "We're in the last elevator, going to the top level. Solaris and Hans are either going to find us up there or wait for us to come down—there's no way out on our own."

There was silence for a moment. Zara looked anxiously at Sam's face as the other passengers in the elevator looked out at the view, pointing and taking photos.

"Jedi?" Sam said, fearing the connection had gone dead.

"There is a way for the two of you to get out, but it'll be tricky," Jedi said. "I'm sending some images to Zara's phone now."

The elevator stopped. They had arrived at the top level, the observation deck nearly a thousand feet above the city, crammed with people taking scenic snapshots.

"Good luck, Sam," Jedi said. "Call me when your feet are back on the grou—"

The line went dead and they were being ushered out of the elevator car. Sam could see the city stretching out below as they got near the edge.

"What do we do?" Zara asked.

Her phone beeped—Jedi's images came through. Sam looked at them wide-eyed, and when Zara saw them, she looked like she was going to throw up.

Jedi's text read:

Change your Stealth Suit to this, glide to a landing on the Seine river and immediately change Suit to flotation device. Oh, and probably best not to swallow any of the river water.

"He cannot be serious!" Zara said, shouting to be heard over the wind which was blowing near gale force.

"Solaris will be in the next elevator up here," Sam said. "We have to move, and move now."

"You're talking about jumping off the Eiffel Tower!" People around them turned to stare at Zara.

"Lower your voice. We're going to have a panic on our hands if people think we're crazy. Look, this is Jedi's idea," Sam said, studying the images closely. "And he knows what he's doing, and he knows it'll work. He wouldn't have suggested it otherwise."

"And can he control the air?" Zara whispered.

Sam understood what she meant—a gust or change in this strong wind could be the end of them.

Then again, if he managed to glide them down safely to the river below . . .

A guide walked by, saying, "James Bond movies have featured several BASE-jumps, including one from the Eiffel Tower in 1985's *A View to a Kill*. A much more successful undertaking than in 1912, when Franz Reichelt, a tailor, jumped from the first deck of the Eiffel Tower testing his invention, his coat forming a crude parachute. Unfortunately, he died in the attempt. If you look online, you can see footage of the police measuring the depth of the hole he made in the earth upon impact . . ."

"We *so* didn't just hear that," Sam said, leading Zara to an empty spot near the fence.

"Sam, I can't!" Zara gasped. Sam saw her face pale in the evening sunlight.

Her phone beeped and she looked down to check her messages.

"My mother!" she said, reading the message on the screen. "She's back in the city! If we just take the next elevator down—"

"Tell her to meet us down there," Sam said, looking down at the ground and then at the cage that wrapped over the viewing area, "on the other side of the river."

"But what if—"

WHOOSH! WHOOSH!

Two jets of fire missed Sam's head by a few inches and melted through the wire mesh fencing.

Sam spun around, instinctively stepping in front of Zara.

Solaris stood with his arm raised at them. Sam locked eyes with him for the briefest of moments before a brave security guard crash-tackled Solaris to the ground.

"Come on!" Sam said, squeezing out of the hole melted

in the fence, grabbing Zara to help her through. "We won't get another chance to do this!"

He helped Zara out onto the ledge.

"We may not get another chance to do *anything!*" she shouted over the panicked screams of the tourists scrambling to get away from the unfolding drama. Sam looked back to see Solaris step over the inert body of the security guard, scattering the crowd as he walked towards them.

"Hang on around my neck," Sam said, maneuvering so that his back was to Zara. "And don't let go!"

WHOOSH!

They threw themselves into the wind.

ALEX

"I couldn't get a warning through to the Academy," Phoebe said in the director's office. "I've tried everything. All channels to the Academy are down."

The director said, "Everything's out?"

"Yes."

"Then we're right," he said. "Stella *is* attacking the Academy—she's jamming all their communications so that they can't call for help. Matrix *must* be working with her!"

Alex's heart skipped a beat.

Matrix had me running a test on blocking their comms. It was all for this . . . I should have known that slimebag was up to no good.

Alex banged his fist against the office wall in frustration. "What can we do?"

"Jack, can you contact Stella?" Phoebe said.

"I've tried, and I'm still trying," the director said, picking up his phone and dialing again. "I've got the Swiss authorities alerted too. They're sending help, but it may be too late."

"What can I do?" Phoebe asked.

"You and Alex gather all the Agents on this list who I know to be loyal," he handed her a printout with names scrolling down the page, "and bring them in here to be briefed. Stella is no longer a member of the Enterprise. She is now one of our enemies."

Phoebe nodded. She and Alex made for the door and the director picked up the phone, making one more desperate attempt to call Stella to somehow persuade her to call off her attack.

The director's office was full with two dozen Agents. The director and Phoebe hastily updated them on Stella's betrayal of the Enterprise and the suspected strike against the Academy. They all listened silently, their expressions dark and glowering.

"We've tried to warn the Academy," Phoebe said to those assembled. "We can't make contact with them or the Dreamer Council, or even any Academy staff worldwide."

Now a murmur ran through the Agents.

"All signals are being jammed in and out of the Academy, sir," a tech confirmed. "Landlines, mobile phones, all radio bands—everything's been either jammed or is off air."

"There's no way of warning them, then?" Alex said.

"It could already be too late . . ." the tech turned to face him directly.

"Contact Geneva again," the director said. "Tell the authorities there to expect casualties, alert the medical staff and get the Swiss authorities on the line again and have them send their teams in—*now!*"

A pair of Agents hustled to the corner of the office and started making urgent phone calls.

"And you can all imagine," the director said to the assembled, "this technical aspect of Stella's assault means that Matrix is involved, although the extent of that involvement we are yet to establish."

"I'll go ask him," a huge mountain of an Agent said, violence in his eyes.

"If only. He's long gone." The director looked to a tech. "Any luck getting Stella on the line?"

"Her comms and those of all the Agents with her have gone silent," the tech replied. "But I've just patched through to the lead helicopter she's acquired. Ready?"

"Put it through on the speakerphone." The director leaned forward at his desk, talking into the receiver. "Stella?"

"I thought you might find me," Stella said.

"What are you *doing?*" Alex could hear the director fight to keep his anger in check.

"You probably know by now," Stella said casually.

"Call it off, Stella," the director said. "Don't do this."

Stella laughed. Alex felt the Agent next to him tense up.

"Why?" the director said.

"What's about to happen at the Academy should have been done a long time ago . . ." Stella replied.

"This is *murder!*" The director was both protesting and pleading at the same time.

"I'm doing what you could never do," Stella spat out. "I'm doing it right now, so you're too late!"

And the line went dead.

"Make sure the Swiss military have responded to our warning!" the director yelled to the Agents manning the phones. "The rest of you come with me to the computer control room!"

The director ran from the room, several Agents with him, Alex following close behind.

At the heavy steel doors to the computer division, an Agent turned from the biometric scanner, his expression worried.

"What?" the director said.

Alex knew before the Agent answered. The doors weren't opening.

"It's been disabled," the Agent replied. "We're locked out."

Matrix!

This is a bad sign, a really bad sign.

EVA

"What are *they*?" Pi said, coming to stand next to Eva and Gabriella. "I mean, I can see they're helicopters—but what are they doing?"

"Xavier?" Eva called up to him, as he hastily joined them at the bottom of the icefall. They could hear the helicopters now, the rotors beating against the air, growing louder with every second as they neared.

"Maybe it's some kind of military exercise they're running somewhere nearby?" Xavier said, catching his breath. "Look at the weaponry they're packing!"

"Nearby *where*?" Eva said, looking around the barren mountains with a knot of dread. She could see rocket pods and machine guns strapped to the sides of the helicopters. Her stomach lurched. "I've got a really bad feeling about this. I think we should raise the alarm and—"

"Look!" Pi said, cutting her off.

They saw a flash from the side of the mountain opposite, near where Eva had been caught in an avalanche, then a streaking into the sky and—

KLAP-BOOM!

"Whoa!" Eva shouted out, her hands flying up to her mouth in shock.

One of the helicopters exploded in the air, a huge ball of scorching fire and black smoke. No sooner had its flaming remains started to fall towards earth as they watched on openmouthed in horror then another flash sprung from the mountain and another missile streaked into the sky—

BOOM!

A second helicopter was hit on the tail rotor and spun wildly out of control, smashing into a ridge and exploding, starting an avalanche of snow and ice.

"What's happening?" Pi screamed.

"Who's shooting?" Gabriella cried.

Eva could now feel the heat carried on the breeze from the explosions.

"I don't know," Eva said, "but we've got to get out of here!"

Alarms began ringing out from the Academy behind them, the noise deafening them.

"Come *on!*" Xavier shouted, leading the way to the rock wall where they climbed their way back up to the terrace, a combined effort of frantic reaching and lifting. Xavier was the last up, hauling himself over the balustrade as—

"They're here, they're attacking us!" Pi shouted. "Take cover!"

SWOOSH!

A missile flashed overhead.

KLAP-BOOM!

A section of the Academy's ancient tile roof plummeted over their heads and fell down the cliff face below. Eva watched as the first four helicopters roared overhead, their machine guns peppering the buildings with bullets, while the two others circled around the mountain.

I hope whoever's out there shoots you all down!

"The evac area is the driveway out front!" Pi shouted.

"I'll lead!" Xavier said, running inside.

In the corridor they saw Jedi disappearing up the stairs.

SMASH!

The whole wall of the corridor before them disintegrated. As if in slow motion, Eva was blown through the air.

SAM

"AAARRGH!" Sam and Zara's screams mingled together as they plunged downward, the breeze now pummeling them like a tornado. The horrified shouts of people in the Eiffel Tower rushed by in a flash.

What have I done? I've just killed us.

Sam forced the panic from his mind and extended his arms, forcing his legs apart into the position on Jedi's instructions. Relief swamped him as he felt their descent immediately slow to a glide as his Stealth Suit held true to Jedi's design of the wing suit.

Nice!

"Argh!" Zara said, not as loud this time. Sam twisted his head back to glimpse Zara's eyes, trying to look as reassuring as he could.

Fortunately, Zara appeared to be over the initial shock. Her grip around Sam's neck remained just as tight, but she tried to give him a smile. It unfortunately looked more like a grimace as she hung on.

Well, I did just make her jump off the Eiffel Tower.

The wind buffeted against Sam's face in a gentle pulse

now. Arms fully outstretched, he leaned right, guiding them in a wide banking arc towards the river far below. They were headed into the wind now, and after a few shaking jinks as Sam adjusted to the conditions, they slowed into a steady flight path.

Sam marveled at this unique view of central Paris, the city spread out below them in a patchwork of avenues and buildings. He could almost feel Zara starting to grin, drinking in the experience.

"Sam!" Zara yelled into his ear. "This is . . . *amazing!*"

"I know!" he said, grinning. He started a slight banking maneuver to the right, so that they'd come to a long gliding landing along the length of the river. "It's awesome!"

WHOOSH!

A ball of fire shot past them, several feet to their right, far enough off not to worry about but close enough to feel the heat as it passed.

The further we get away, the less likely he'll be able to hit us.

WHOOSH!

That jet was even further away.

So that's the edge of his range, Sam thought without needing to look back.

"Go faster!" Zara screamed in Sam's ear.

"I can't!" he replied. "We have to slow as much as we can for landing!"

WHOOSH!

"Wow!" Sam said, blinking against the heat from the close shot.

He's not trying to hit us, Sam realized, seeing the pattern in the shots which kept Sam banking away from the slow-moving Seine below. *He's trying to steer me away from the river and towards the roads . . . he's making sure we don't get a clean getaway when we land.*

Far below, people who had been oblivious to the midair drama above them were now looking up, pointing. Their attention turned to gasps of horror when fireballs shot through the air.

"Sam?" Zara leaned into his ear to shout. "*Sam!*"

"Yeah—I know," Sam yelled back. Their descent was *too* slow. They were covering too *much* ground. At this rate, they'd overshoot not only the river, but the open grassy area too.

"You better do something," Zara said, shifting her weight—which made Sam veer wildly left, then as she shifted back to compensate, her grip around his neck started to choke him.

"Za-ra, can't . . . breathe . . ."

Her grip relaxed and she was still. "Pardon!" she called out.

Sam sucked in the cool air and adjusted his wing suit.

"Sam . . . we're headed for . . ."

"I know!"

The far side of a bridge, crossing the river.

"But—"

"We'll be OK," Sam said. "Close your eyes."

"I'm closing them!"

Sam aimed for the bridge, with no more than ten seconds before they would land. Among the cars, three buses were in convoy across the bridge. The furthest away had an open top and was full of tourists. The next two had smooth tops, potential landing spots. They were moving in the same direction as their descent. Sam hoped they could land on one doing about the same speed—hopefully giving them a softer landing. Sam aimed for the middle bus.

"Five seconds!" Sam yelled back over his shoulder. He felt Zara tense.

As they neared the middle bus he pushed his feet down slightly and his angle of descent straightened a little. They slowed to a similar speed to the bus.

Horns blared in the traffic below.

The bus braked and slowed down further.

Sam pulled his arms close to his body, picking up a few yards of forward speed, and then dropped his feet again.

They passed over the third bus, its smooth white roof a runway, and Sam closed his arms and legs to speed up.

All the traffic seemed to come to a sudden halt.

The second bus flashed under them.

"Oh no!"

Sam opened his arms and legs, slowing—

WHACK!

They hit the third bus hard, the air knocked out of Sam from Zara's full weight resting on his back. They skidded down the central aisle, tourists jumping back in their seats. Sam thumped his head on the front board and looked up into the stunned faces of a family of tourists. Zara rolled off Sam, gasping to catch her breath. A little boy jumped out of his shocked father's arms and shouted, "Do it again, mister!"

They pulled each other to their feet as a cluster of faces came towards them, taking pictures and offering assistance and congratulations.

Do they think we were doing some kind of stunt?

"No photos, please!" Sam said in desperation, thinking of his face plastered all over the news again. But it was too late.

"Come, Sam," Zara said as she dragged Sam down the stairs to scattered applause. She called out behind them, "Merci, merci!"

The bus was slowing to round a corner and they came to a stop in the traffic. Zara barked a few hysterical words in French to the unsuspecting driver and he opened the door. They jumped out and ran along the street, stopping once they reached the safety of the sidewalk. Sam put his hands on his knees, doubling over, fighting for air.

"What'd you say to him?" Sam asked.

"That I was going to be sick," Zara said, her hands on her stomach. "And it was no lie."

She doubled over and threw up over the edge of the bridge. She turned back to face Sam, looking pale and frightened.

It won't take them long to get back down here—I have to keep her moving.

A loud and long honk of a car horn made Sam turn around in fright. *Not already!*

"My mother!" Zara said, running through the gridlock to the other side of the bridge. She held the door open for Sam, who took a final look up at the Eiffel Tower and collapsed into the backseat of the car.

34

"**P**apa just sent a message," Zara said, reading her phone. "He has some minor injuries, nothing serious."

"That *is* good news. Tell him we are arriving in Amboise," Zara's mom, Aubree, said as she drove. "We'll be at Clos Lucé in minutes."

Zara turned to Sam. "He and your Guardians were able to escape. They are all right also."

"Great, thank you," Sam said. They had been traveling in the car for just over two hours but he couldn't help but stare out the rear window, wondering who would be coming behind them.

"You ready, Sam?" Zara asked over her shoulder.

"Yeah," he replied. In truth, he was anxious and worried. The entire car trip he'd tried to reach the Academy again, but all the lines were down. He didn't know anything more about the Professor and the Council. And he didn't know whether Solaris or Hans were still after them.

On the plus side, he was traveling with an Enterprise Agent, which meant if there was any Enterprise trouble headed their way, they'd know about it. He looked at his phone again, willing someone to call and update him.

"Any word from your friends?" Aubree asked Sam, stealing a glance his way in the rearview mirror.

"Nothing," Sam replied. The last he'd heard from Jedi was the crackly connection via Zara's phone. "At the very least, I'd like to tell Jedi about our jump from the Tower."

"I cannot bring myself to believe we just did that. It was terrifying, non?" Zara said. "Let's not do it again, OK?"

"Least you had your eyes closed," Sam said, passing back her phone on which he'd been reading up about Clos Lucé. "I had to watch the whole thing."

"Sam, you can handle what's ahead?" Aubree asked, pulling the car up to the side of the road.

"Yes," Sam said. "I think so."

Aubree nodded. "This is as far as I go."

Zara said, "Can't you come with us?"

"No, ma cherie, I'm sorry." She took Zara's hands in her own and kissed Zara's cheek.

"But—you're my mother . . ."

"And she's also an Enterprise Agent," Sam said. "She knows what she's doing."

"And when you two are in the clear and far away, I will call in and report that the two of you disappeared before we could meet."

"Aubree, thank you," Sam said. "You've done a good thing."

Aubree smiled. Zara sniffled away tears.

"Zara, I have a job to do," Aubree said. "I must stop your pursuers as best I can."

"What about the police?" Zara said. "Then you can come with us."

"This is our battle and the police don't understand what's at stake," she said. "Besides, they can't lock these people up until they catch them in the act or have proof. They're so wealthy and powerful, they'd be out of custody immediately."

"Please—"

"I've dreamed my role in this," she said, smiling. "Don't worry, darling. You and Sam will be fine."

Aubree passed her an antique dream catcher charm, which looked a lot like the one Lora had given Sam.

"This was my mother's," Aubree said. "It'll bring you luck."

"But you need it," Zara argued.

"I'll be fine," her mother insisted.

"How do you know?"

"I know," Aubree said, her hand reassuring on her daughter's face.

Sam stood and watched as Aubree drove away. Zara mopped up her tears with her sleeve.

Where is she going? To Paris, to collect her husband? Or will she lead the chase someplace else?

Sam considered if the Enterprise had a way of tracking her, as the Academy could track him so long as he wore his dream catcher. Maybe she was leaving them to do this themselves while leading Stella away?

"We have to keep moving," Sam resolved, walking through the last of the day's shadows cast by the imposing castle-like Château d'Amboise.

Zara remained where she was, watching as her mother's car disappeared around a corner.

Sam walked back to her, but before he could say anything of comfort or persuasion, another car was coming. He grabbed Zara and pushed her down behind a wall with him. They peered out as the car drove past. Sam saw the face of the guy from the Council in the rear window. Mac had arrived.

EVA

Eva lay on her side, bells ringing inside her head. Pi's face was close to hers and he was yelling something at her but the words had no sound.

Have I gone deaf?

She was helped to her feet by Xavier. Gabriella had blood running from her ears. The hallway ahead was gone, the open expanse of the cliffs extending below the cantilevered structure. The remnants of the ceiling's wooden beams were on fire.

Pi led the way in the opposite direction towards a steep set of stairs. As the four of them ascended, Eva's hearing returned, low notes at first, and then all the range came blasting back. She realized the ringing was not just in her mind or damaged eardrums, but it was the Academy's evacuation alarm.

"Through here!" Pi pushed open the door onto the grand entrance hall. Only one wall remained, the rest were piles of rubble. Debris was kicked up as helicopters buzzed directly overhead. They ran to take cover at the last wall.

"Over here!" Lora yelled.

She was with a group of Guardians behind a makeshift barricade, firing at their attackers with an assortment of weapons.

Eva and the others ran close to the ground and joined the remaining Academy staff.

"Keep your heads down and stay behind this wall!" Lora commanded them.

Eva nodded, cowering down low behind the stonework.

"There are still three aircraft," a Guardian said to Lora. "And we're out of ground-to-air missiles."

Lora looked grim.

Just then, a new sound cut through the mountain air. It was a snowmobile, tearing hard and fast up the driveway. In the distance was an apparition Eva had seen before—*Tobias!*

And strapped to his back, a rocket launcher.

Eva turned to see Pi running towards a fallen Guardian who still had a loaded rocket launcher next to him. "Pi! Get down! Tobias is coming!"

Pi was already far across the hall, out in the open.

A helicopter loosed a missile.

WHOOSH!

Pi dived for cover behind a pile of smoldering stones.

Too late.

KLAP-BOOM!

The explosion hit just in front of the stones, right at Pi's heels as he jumped from the ground. Eva felt time slow as Pi was sent cartwheeling through the air and landed with a dull thud on a bank of snow.

No!

The helicopter still buzzed overhead but not caring for her own skin, Eva ran out, legs pumping hard. She slid down to grab the launcher from the dead Guardian, spinning around to catch the helo in the optical sights. The helicopter banked around for another attack, firing its machine guns at the walled position where her friends were.

The eyepiece beeped that it had locked on.

Eva did not hesitate. She pulled the trigger.

WHOOSH!

The missile shot out from the launcher, the plume of smoke streaking into the sky. Eva looked up to see—

BOOM!

A direct hit. Eva turned away as the fireball enveloped the attack helicopter which plummeted to the ground with an earsplitting mechanical screech. Another explosion rocked the air above her as Tobias took down another helicopter.

Eva had eyes only for Pi as she sprinted towards him. She fell to her knees next to him. "Pi . . ." she said.

He was on his back, his arms and legs at odd angles,

blood staining the snow. His eyes opened and when he saw her face, he smiled.

"Pi—hang in there!" Eva said, then yelled towards the others, "Quick! Help!"

He continued to smile, his expression calm and quiet.

"Pi, just wait for help," Eva pleaded, seeing his eyes falter, his chest heaving jaggedly with breath. "Just wait, OK? You'll be OK."

"No . . . I think I have to go now."

"Pi, no, *please*," Eva begged, her hand to the side of his face, "please, be strong. Help will be here soon."

Pi smiled and his gaze was steady.

"I'm going to dream forever," he said. Then his body went limp.

36

SAM

Sam and Zara stayed hidden in the shadows of the trees as Mac sped by without seeing them.

"Who was that?" she asked.

"A guy from the Dreamer Council," Sam said.

"That's great!" Zara said, then added, "Wait, why do we hide from him?"

"Because I'm not sure whose side he's on," Sam said, quickly explaining Mac's revolt at the Council meeting.

"Maybe he's here to help?" Zara said, falling into step next to Sam as they raced across the road to Clos Lucé.

"I'm not convinced about that," Sam said.

"You think he followed us here from Paris?" she asked.

"Maybe . . . I mean, how else could he have known where to come?" Sam stopped, looked at the imposing chateau before them. "But if he's headed to da Vinci's workshop, he'll beat us there!"

"No," Zara said. "There's another way in—a shortcut."

The tunnel from the stone chateau to da Vinci's workshop ran from the basement cellar.

"And you knew about this, how?" Sam asked as they ran through the passageway.

"A tour," Zara replied.

"Really?"

"This was the royal chateau, and Francis I had da Vinci here as his guest," she said. "The grounds and museum are full of da Vinci models. My dad has brought me here many times. Oh, no," Zara said at the bottom of stone stairs. The passageway ended at a steel gate which was secured with an old lock.

"What's wrong?" Sam said from behind Zara.

She pointed to the gate. "Of course, it was open during the tour."

"Just a sec, I've got an idea," Sam replied, putting the edge of the Stealth Suit's sleeve into the door hinges. "Stand back a bit."

Sam turned the sleeve of his suit into the arm of a puffer jacket, filling the gap. Nothing. The door didn't budge.

"So much for that great idea," Sam said, stepping back from the door. "We're going to have to go back and around to the workshop above us."

"Or not . . . it is hardly a modern masterpiece," Zara said.

"What?"

Zara pulled a hairpin from her hair and bent it, jiggling it around inside the lock.

Holding his phone's light steady, Sam watched as Zara wrestled with the lock—

CLICK.

The lock sprang open, and with a few nudges, the door creaked open on rusty hinges.

"Paris, *represent!*" Sam smiled. Zara gave him a quick mock curtsey.

"Follow me," she commanded as they went in.

Old concrete stairs led upward, the arched brick tunnel surrounds opening up. At the top of the next stairs was an iron gate, this time thankfully unlocked, and they went through into the basement level of da Vinci's final home and workshop.

"This must be for storage," Zara said, weaving her way through boxes of cleaning products and canned goods for the tourist cafe above.

"Zara," Sam said, the little light between them illuminating the room. "It's up to you now, your dream."

She nodded.

"Can you remember where we have to go?"

"Yes."

In a bedroom which Sam guessed was da Vinci's, Zara went straight to the ornate fireplace. They moved quietly, careful not to make a sound to alert anyone else in the dark house.

There came the sound of breaking glass downstairs, echoing loudly in the silence.

Sam froze.

Zara staggered forward in fright and bumped her head on the mantelpiece. She stifled a cry as a crystal ball displayed on top bumped off its holder and rolled along headed for the edge.

Sam lunged for it—

His fingers touched the crystal's smooth edge but it raced by and shattered on the floor.

Zara looked at Sam with eyes wide with fear. For a moment all was quiet.

Maybe they didn't hear it?

Heavy footfalls were coming up the stairs.

"Zara!" Sam said, racing to shut the bedroom door. "If you're gonna find anything, make it quick!"

Zara went to the fireplace and began feeling into the nooks and crannies.

At the door, Sam took the stun grenade from his pack, pulled the pin and tossed it down the hall, then slammed the door shut and leaned against it.

"Cover your ears!" Sam shouted, watching as she did so.

BANG!

Even with his hands over his ears, the explosion was near-deafening, the blinding white light that flashed under the door enough to completely light up their room for one eerie second.

"One moment!" Zara said, as her finger ran across the filigree design, searching, remembering.

CLICK.

"Got it!" Zara said.

Sam rushed back to her as the side of the stone fireplace swung open like a door, the opening big enough to squeeze through sideways.

"Can we close it from inside?" Sam asked. They searched the inside wall, looking for some kind of lever.

"Here!" Zara touched a hidden latch, the panel closing behind them.

"That should buy us some time," Sam whispered.

By the light of their phones, they could see they were in a small square brick room with no adornments and, worryingly, no other way out. The room was bare.

"Is this how it was in your dream?" Sam whispered.

Zara remained silent as she looked around, closely inspecting the brickwork for something that Sam could not see.

Through the tiny cracks in the hidden door panel, Sam could hear voices in the bedroom beyond. As he worried that the light from their phones might be visible—

"Sam!" Zara whispered.

Standing next to her on the other side of the room, he could see that she had found a brick that was worn smooth. Zara rested the fingers of one hand into what were slight indentations and pushed.

The brick moved in, the whole wall sliding across into a hidden cavity behind it.

"That's *cool*," Sam said.

Zara went first, walking down steep stone stairs.

We might be the first people to walk on these stairs since da Vinci. Man!

They went down a long flight of stairs, ending in another, slightly larger room. The end wall was roughly chiseled rock with two side walls covered in wooden shelves full of dust and cobwebs. Blowing them away, Sam found tools, bowls, trowels, jars of powders and pigments.

"Da Vinci's workshop?" Sam asked hopefully.

"More like his toolshed," Zara replied. "And more storage."

"This *isn't* where we need to be?"

"No . . ."

"So where?" Sam asked. There were no doors to be seen. He banged on the far wall. It was solid rock.

"I didn't dream this room," Zara said. "I went through the fireplace, it was a bit hazy—then I was in the other room."

Sam knew that the dreams did that. They didn't show every detail and often jumped from one moment to another. Zara looked over the contents of the shelves. There was nothing around but the rough-hewn rock walls. The cobwebs in front of Sam shifted slightly. He looked closer.

"There's a breeze!" Sam said. "The air is being sucked upstairs and out the seams of the hidden door above."

"From where?"

"Exactly!" Sam felt around the shelves in front of him. He could feel the rock wall behind and it was smooth. At the end of the shelving, there was a crack where the air was filtering through. "It's here."

Sam pulled at the shelving but it wouldn't budge. He tried lifting it, pushing it, prying it—nothing.

Zara began clearing the shelves and turned to Sam with a smile.

There, set in the smooth stone face, was an etched diagram of interlocking Gears.

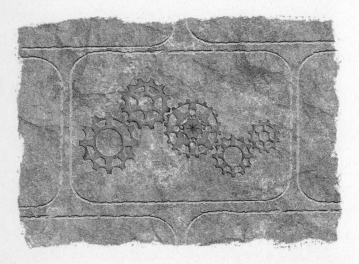

"That's part of the Bakhu . . ." Sam said. He snapped a photo of it on his phone. The center of the diagram, the largest of the Gears, was inset with a brass disk.

"And here, I think, we need that special key of yours . . ." Zara said.

Sam took the key from around his neck, and the pointed star-shaped end fitted neatly into the brass lock. He turned it carefully.

There was a sharp *CLONK!* and a grinding noise as the shelves opened out.

Each side of the floor-to-ceiling shelves was hinged and they opened in the middle.

Suddenly a lion appeared out of the darkness, roaring as it came at Sam.

"Argh!" Sam dropped his phone and fell back in horror.

The beast stopped, and gave off a small ticking sound where it was stuck in place, its forward legs twitching.

"It's mechanical," Zara said, looking closely at it. "I was going to tell you I saw a lion attack us in my dream, but it sounded too weird."

"Next time, maybe you could warn me?" Sam said, embarrassed as he got up and dusted himself off.

Sam picked up his phone and in its weak light he checked out the lion. It had been preserved, so for all outwards appearances resembled a real lion, only this one had an open panel on the side and mechanical workings inside.

"Da Vinci made this?" Sam said.

"I've seen a modern replica," Zara said, stepping over the threshold into the next hidden room. "Oh *wow* . . ."

"What?" Sam walked in behind her and his jaw dropped

at what he saw. Parts of machines were everywhere, on benches and on walls, along with pulleys and lifts and building materials. Plans and papers were strewn on the ground. What looked like an old space capsule sat in the center of the room—

"That's da Vinci's design for a tank," Zara said. "And that," she said pointing to a large object hanging from the roof, "a kind of helicopter."

"This is amazing. And a bit surreal. It's like we're in a movie about da Vinci. Have you ever seen so much of his stuff in one place?" Sam marveled.

"Da Vinci's secret workshop," Zara said, awestruck. "Even in my dream, I couldn't believe it. If my father could see this now . . ."

"I can just imagine. I know a few other people who would lose their minds to see this stuff. But for now we have to find what we came for," Sam said. "I know it's tough, but try to stay focused."

"OK, of course," Zara said.

"Where was it in your dream?" Sam prompted.

Zara was way ahead of him. She went over to a desk in the far corner. "Yes, this is right. OK, now . . ." She opened a drawer, hesitating, "No, next one." She knelt down on the dusty floor and pulled at the handle of the larger drawer underneath.

At first it jammed and she exhaled quietly as she teased it open, bit by bit. As Sam stood watching, she eventually had it open, reaching in to pull out a wooden box, swathed inside a large cloth bag. It was the size of a shoe box.

Zara wiped her sleeve over the lid, smearing away the dirt and grime of hundreds of years, revealing notations and symbols etched all over the brass fittings. She paused, looking up at Sam. He nodded.

Do it.

Gingerly, Zara cracked open the box, the hinges squeaking as it opened fully. Inside, lit by their lights, was a geared crankshaft.

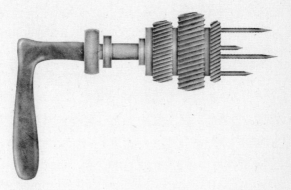

Zara nodded. She'd found what she was looking for.

"This box . . ." Sam said, pulling back the side of the bag to reveal the full box. "This isn't just where the next piece is—this is *it*. It's the casing for the Bakhu Machine itself!"

Yes! Maybe we can win.

Before either of them could say another word, an almighty explosion rang out.

"They're blasting their way through the fireplace!" Sam said, loading the box into his backpack as they ran back. "Help me shut the bookcase. We can hide in here!"

Try as they might, they couldn't work out the mechanism to close the two halves of the bookcase doors.

"Plan B!" Sam said, running back into the workshop.

"What's plan B?"

"Another way out."

"But there's no—?"

"The breeze, the wind that's being sucked upstairs," Sam said. "It means that there's another way out down here."

At the far wall of the room was a large wooden door with a heavy metal bolt slid across it.

This door was only ever meant to be opened from this side.

Sam and Zara heaved the bolt out of the way, groaning with the exertion. They found a narrow corridor beyond it that went further than they could see by their small lights.

Leaning against the wall next to the door was a bicycle, but not like any Sam had ever ridden before.

"I don't believe it!" Zara gasped. "Most da Vinci scholars think his bicycle plans were a forgery or a fake. But look— here it is!"

"Well, fake or not, let's go!" Sam said, and climbed onto the odd-looking prototype bicycle. Zara didn't wait to be asked again and delicately balanced herself on the wooden crossbar, lighting the way with her phone.

Sam pushed off and was grateful for the sloping floor that let them pick up speed.

"The tunnel starts curving left!" Zara said.

"How do I steer?" Sam called out. "There's no steering!"

"What?"

"This bike can't turn. Some genius he was!" Sam yelled.

"Then lean to the left," Zara shouted. "Now!"

As they rounded the curve, the tunnel narrowed so

that the wooden handlebars were practically touching the walls.

OK, we can do this. We're escaping on an antique bike with no steering.

What wasn't OK, what was frightening, was the floor beneath them. It was now shooting downward at an ever-increasing rate.

"I can't stop!" Sam said as he tried to use his feet to slow them down. "There's no brakes!"

"I hear running water!" Zara screamed.

"Arghhh!" they screamed in unison.

Before Sam could try to stop them, they were airborne.

SPLASH!

37

ALEX

The director bypassed the security panel and rewired the circuit, sparks flying. The heavy steel doors to the computer labs hissed open.

Thick dark smoke poured out.

"Get a medical team in here!" the director said to the Agent by his side. He rushed inside and broke a thin glass panel by the door. He pulled down the red lever inside. There was a loud roaring noise followed by rushing jets of white vapor and the flashing of red lights. The smoke was sucked out from the room by huge fans recessed into the ceiling.

"Shiva!" Alex raced to his friend, who was on his back on the ground. "Shiva?"

Shiva slowly regained consciousness and looked up at Alex.

"I tried to stop him…" Shiva said. "Help me—help me up."

Alex and the director helped Shiva to his feet as several medics rushed into the room and began attending to the other semiconscious computer techs.

"What happened, Shiva?" the director asked.

"He—Matrix, he left, and then came back with a few field Agents, all wearing masks. They set off gas or something."

"I want Matrix found," the director barked to an Agent, who hustled out of the room.

"I saw him take the hard drives," Shiva said. "And I saw him . . . I saw him . . ."

"What?" Alex said.

"He checked in on Stella, in the field," Shiva said. "She's leading a full-scale assault somewhere."

"The Academy," Alex said. "We know."

Shiva staggered against a chair and Alex reached out to take his weight.

"Let's get you to the medical bay," the director said, taking one of Shiva's arms over his shoulder and Alex taking the other. "I'm going to need you up to full speed ASAP."

"What for?" Shiva said.

"Because you're my new Matrix," he said with a determined tone.

"But there's nothing left to work with," Shiva said.

"We've got a backup site," the director said, and Shiva looked surprised at the revelation. "Neither Stella nor Matrix know about it. Everything on our computers is backed up there."

"Where?" Shiva asked.

"Amsterdam," the director said. "Soon as you're up to it, we'll get you on a flight there to activate the site."

"One request?" Shiva said.

"Sure."

"Alex comes too."

The director hesitated but nodded. "OK."

"Thanks," Alex said.

"Oh," Shiva said, "and one more thing. Don't call me Matrix."

Alex grimaced as they walked Shiva towards the door. He glanced at a computer station as they passed by. "Hey, were these on before?"

As they looked around the room, every screen powered up, casting an eerie glow in the emergency lighting.

"What the . . ?" Shiva muttered.

Dozens of screens lit up, each showing the same image. Dozens and dozens of skulls and crossbones. Matrix's laugh boomed from every monitor as the skulls disappeared. What replaced them was even more frightening. It was a countdown clock. The red light flickered as the echoing ticking filled the room. Five minutes and counting.

"Everybody out of the building!" the director yelled as they started running for the door. "Sound the alarm—total evac, NOW!"

EVA

Eva gently laid Pi down on the ground. She covered him with a blanket, then turned from his still body on the snow, not even trying to stem her tears, and walked slowly to the others.

Above, the sky was clear, all the helicopters but one were burning wrecks on the mountains. The one that got away was a speck getting smaller in the distance with every passing second.

Eva saw Tobias hurry back and forth, treating injured Guardians and students. Lora was on the phone, now working, calling in emergency response teams. Eva turned around to see Xavier and Gabriella manning a fire hose, working alongside a smattering of Guardians to save what was left of the Academy's mountaintop campus, now in burning ruins.

Eva stumbled towards Tobias. All she could hear were the sounds of people trying to make their way clear of the rubble, calling out to each other, crying, screaming. Students emerged from the smoke, some walking, others limping or being carried.

"Pi . . . he's d—" Eva broke down as Tobias reached for her and pulled her into his arms.

"I'm so sorry, Eva," he sighed. "We don't know how many we've lost. Too many . . ."

"What can I do?" Eva rallied and looked around.

"Here," he said, showing her how to place some gauze wadding gently against the eyes of an injured Guardian while he unpacked a bandage.

"I don't understand how you're here. Why'd you hide on the mountain all this time?" Eva asked.

"I just knew it was what I had to do," Tobias said as he wrapped the bandage around the Guardian's head.

"Had to?"

"So that I would be here, today, to do what I did."

"All those nights out in the cold . . ." Eva looked across to where he'd been living out in the snow, a sentinel watching over the Academy.

"Were all worth it because of this."

"You knew this would happen?"

"No," Tobias said, standing. "I just dreamed that it was where I had to be, and that I was alone, waiting for the moment when I could help."

"And you saved me from freezing to death on the mountain?" Eva asked.

Tobias nodded.

Eva looked around at the destruction. Fires still blazed, the wounded were being looked after as best as could be managed with their limited supplies. Lora came off the phone and walked over. She and Tobias hugged in a tight embrace.

"Are you OK?" Lora asked Eva.

"Yeah," Eva replied, looking over to Pi. "He's gone . . ."

Lora pulled Eva into the shared embrace. "I'm so sorry."

Eva choked back tears. They were all in this together—they were family now, brought together even more through their shared grief.

"What do we do next?" Eva asked, sniffing away more tears and gathering resolve.

"We look after each other," Lora sighed. "And then we must carry on."

"What—what about everyone who died?" Eva said.

"There will be a time for revenge, Eva," Tobias said darkly.

She looked at the tiny dot of the helicopter in the distance, then over to her friends battling the flames and knew that none of them would ever be the same.

In the rising smoke of the fire, Eva wondered if Sam was faring any better.

I hope so because we can't help you now.

SAM

"We must be close to the Chateau d'Amboise," Zara said, shivering on the stone step. "This is the Loire river."

Sam looked out the iron storm water grate. Thanks to their unexpected dip, Zara's phone was toast and his waterproof one had only minutes of battery left due to running the flashlight app. Soon they'd be in darkness but for the moonlit night outside.

"How do we get out?" Sam asked. The bars were thick and solid, like those of a prison cell.

"We swim," Zara said, dropping back into the water. "We must go now, they are coming."

Sam watched as Zara disappeared into the dark water.

"Zara?"

A moment later she emerged on the other side of the iron grate.

"Swim under!" she called out to him.

Sam dropped into the water, took a deep breath, and dived down. He felt his way in the dark. Not far below the waterline, the ends of the metal grate had rusted away. He pulled himself under, squeezing his backpack with him and pushed off, swimming out to Zara.

"Across to the other riverbank," Zara said, pushing off.

"OK," Sam replied, following her lead.

"We are on a small island," Zara said, as they got their breath back on the grassy bank. "We can take this bridge across the next half of the Loire and find a telephone."

Zara fell silent, staring behind Sam, who turned—

Mac grabbed him around the throat and lifted him to his feet, three thugs looming behind him. Sam tried to fight him off, but his grip was too strong.

"So, Sam . . ." Mac said, grinning. "What have you got for me?"

Sam kicked Mac hard as he could in the shins. Mac grunted with pain and his grip loosened a little. A thug stepped in to pin Sam's arms as another took hold of Zara, fighting to gain control of her as she resisted.

"Ah, good, you've both got a little fight in you," Mac said. He turned to the remaining thug. "Check the kid's bag."

"What did you do to the Council?" Sam asked.

"They got what they deserved," Mac said.

"You killed them?"

"Killed? No, that's not my style," Mac said, smiling. "They just got roughed up a little."

"Hey, boss," one of the thugs said. "They've got the box."

"Ah," Mac said. "So you were right after all, Sam—it's some kind of da Vinci device."

"You'll find you're wrong about a lot of things," Sam fired back.

"Perhaps, but I doubt it," Mac said. "You see, *my* ancestors are descended from another famous Dreamer in history—Nostradamus."

"Did he predict *this* for you?" Sam said, using his jujitsu training to pull free, kicking Mac hard in the groin. Mac recoiled in agony, Sam flipping him hard onto his back with another move.

CRACK!

Sam was knocked to the ground by the butt of a dart gun. He clutched at the back of his head and saw stars. As his vision cleared he saw Zara struggling against a thug while the other put his pistol away. He was still holding the Bakhu box.

"Sam . . ." Mac hissed as he got to his feet. "I was going to make this easy on you, but now—now, it's gonna *hurt*."

Mac moved forward towards Sam, ready to attack. Sam braced for a blow that never came. As he turned to see what had happened, a bolt of fire flashed before his eyes.

Mac's thugs were gone.

Not completely gone, Sam was disgusted to see. They were each a pile of red-hot remains on the grassy bank of the river, reduced to almost nothing by Solaris' fire.

Solaris walked into view from the shadows under the bridge.

"Mac . . ." Solaris said, his metallic voice echoing through his mask. "You've been a bad boy, Mac."

"You . . ." Mac cowered back against a boulder, then towards the ground as if his crouched stance could protect him. "I didn't know you'd be here."

"Oh, I'm everywhere." Solaris reached down and pressed the barrel of his fire weapon onto Mac's forehead, sizzling in a burned ring of charred flesh. "You always were an idiot," he said, and Mac fainted, either from the pain of the burn or the shock, perhaps both. "*And* weak."

Solaris turned to Sam and Zara, now holding on to each other. Sam stepped in front of Zara, squaring off, struggling to breathe normally after Mac's crushing stranglehold.

"Sam, Sam . . ." Solaris said, chiding him, stalking playfully around like a cat with a cornered mouse. "Who's your little friend?" Solaris picked up the backpack containing the Bakhu box and Zara's Gear.

"No!" Zara yelled. "You can't have it!"

As Sam went to run at Solaris, sirens sounded and red and blue lights flashed on the road behind them. Sam spun around.

The police? I could use a little help here.

He turned back to Solaris but he was already gone, taking great strides across the riverbank and out of reach.

No! Not another Gear . . . and the box!

Before Sam could react, figures emerged from the water in front of them, ghostly in the near-darkness. They were the ones who'd been behind them in da Vinci's workshop and followed them here, swimming across the water. They had lain in wait to see what happened with Mac and Solaris before making their move.

It was Hans' treacherous German Guardians.

"Run! To the police!" Sam yelled as he and Zara scrambled up the bank to the road beyond. The flashing lights from the car blinded them as they ran towards it.

A figure stepped out, laughing as he said, "And so we meet again, Sam. How wonderful."

"So what, now you've got the police on your payroll, Hans?" Sam said defiantly.

"Of course," Hans sneered. "You'd be amazed at what, and who, money can buy."

Sam looked around desperately.

"I do hope you're not thinking of rushing off anywhere," Hans said. "I have some very sad news for you. The Academy is no more. Oh yes," he added in reply to Sam's shocked expression. "Blown into dust, no doubt by our mutual friend, Solaris, and his allies."

The German Guardians were on the road now, fanning out and surrounding Sam and Zara on all sides.

"There's no one to come rescue you now, Sam. You're on your own."